DEATH'S DOOR

THE IMMORTAL DESCENDANTS: BALTIMORE MYSTERIES

APRIL WHITE

The Immortal Descendants Series
Marking Time
Tempting Fate
Changing Nature
Waging War
Cheating Death

The Immortal Descendants: Baltimore Mysteries
Death's Door

The Baker Street Series
An Urchin of Means

The Cipher Security Series
Code of Conduct
Code of Honor

This is a work of fiction. All of the characters, organizations, and events portrayed in this novel are either products of the author's imagination or are used fictitiously.

Edited by Angela Houle
Cover Design by Edward Gorsuch
Cover images by Shutterstock

ISBN 978-1-946161-16-1
Library of Congress Control Number: 2020909632

First American edition, May, 2020

“It is by no means an irrational fancy that,
in a future existence, we shall look upon what we think
our present existence, as a dream.”
~ Edgar Allan Poe

TABLE OF CONTENTS

Author's Note

This Immortal Descendants: Baltimore Mysteries novella stands alone and can be read without knowing anything at all about the Immortals or their Descendants. It is set in the same world as the five books of the Immortal Descendants series and the peripheral Baker Street Mysteries, but need not be read in that order.

If this is your first introduction to that world, welcome.

CHAPTER ONE

Alexandra "Ren" Reynolds

The first time I met Edgar Allan Poe was the night he walked into my bar.

That might not seem strange in Baltimore, where Poe was practically a Halloween mascot, but my instincts rang like church bells, warning that everything about this man was from the nineteenth century. He wore a rumpled, black, hand-stitched suit with a dingy white neck-cloth tied over a high collared shirt. His trademark black hair was matted, his mustache too thick and unevenly trimmed, and he stank of corn whiskey and unwashed wool. To most people, Edgar Allan Poe in a twenty-first-century bar was just a guy in a costume.

I wasn't most people.

I had just opened The Door, the bar I owned in Fells Point, and had served a couple of regular customers their first drinks when Poe stumbled inside. His head swiveled owlishly, as though his eyes

1

couldn't focus on any one point, at least not until they found me. The moment they locked on mine they widened slightly, right before they rolled back in his head. He crumpled to the floor in a puddle of black wool and melted bones.

"Damn it," I muttered under my breath. I had a feeling my life was about to get complicated. I threw the bar towel into the sink and rushed to kneel by his head.

"You need help, Ren?" Paul asked. He and Marla lived in one of the Douglass Place houses, and they used The Door like an extension of their living room.

"It's okay, I got him," I said. Poe's eyelids fluttered and his chest rose and fell with each breath, so at least he wasn't dead. Yet? Or was it 'again,' considering that Edgar Allan Poe had been dead for something like a hundred and seventy years. We were still a month away from Halloween, and even then not many could pull off a perfect impersonation of the odd-looking, unmistakable man, so the chances of him being remarked upon were high.

I felt for the pulse in his neck and found a strong, steady beat. His skin had the waxen, sweaty look of someone who was likely to vomit in his unconscious state. He groaned and sat up, so I helped him to his feet. "Paul," I called to the man whose conversations with his wife inevitably turned to gossip about the neighbors, "I'm going to help him to the bathroom. Will you watch the bar for me? Macey will be here in a minute, and I want to make sure this guy's okay."

"Sure thing, honey. We've got you covered."

I threw Poe's arm over my shoulder and walked him to the back. We'd nearly made it to the bathroom when his knees gave way again and he went down. Realizing the bathroom was too much to manage, I turned and dragged Poe with me into the storeroom. I lowered him to the floor and rolled him to his side so he wouldn't choke on the inevitable vomit. Then I stood and looked down at him.

What was Edgar Allan Poe doing in my bar?

I could leave him there to sleep off the alcohol, but I knew that both Macey and I would be in and out of the room all night, and I didn't relish the explanations or the experience. I needed to keep him safe and out of sight until he could tell me how and why he was here, so I stepped over him and got to work shifting boxes off a metal rack. The rack looked like a built-in storage shelving unit, but where the post met the wall, a clever hinge allowed the empty rack to swing open, revealing the nearly invisible seam of a door hidden in the wall behind it.

It had been a long time since I'd opened that door, but the key was still on the rack, and the lock turned easily enough. I flipped the switch inside the room, and an ornate wall sconce flickered to life. The bulbs were old and looked like candles, but the light hadn't been used much, so I wasn't too worried it would burn out and leave Poe in the dark.

I debated dropping the twin mattress that lay propped against the wall, but decided it would be easier to clean vomit off the floor, and the early October night was warm enough that his wool suit would be adequate for insulation. The space between the walls was the width of the twin mattress and twice as long, so I was able to drag Poe's unconscious body in and position him on his side without kicking him more than two or three times. When he was as safe as I could make him, I left the space I'd always just called 'the nest' and pulled the door closed behind me. Then I pushed the empty rack back in place and replaced the full cases with empty ones, surprised at how easily the old habits came back.

I quickly checked my reflection in the mirror I'd hung by the door, looking for evidence that I'd just dragged an unconscious man into a hidden room. What I saw was the same woman I'd seen in mirrors since I started looking – dark, unruly curls, brown skin that still had remnants of a summer tan, and the green eyes I'd inherited from my white father. My parents had been dead a long time, but I could still see the echoes of my mother's serious expression on my own face, especially when I was determined. That determination stared back at me from the mirror when I squared my shoulders, took a deep breath, and pasted a smile on my face as if Edgar Allan Poe were not passed out behind my storeroom wall.

"Ren?" Macey called from the back. "Sorry I'm late. I'll be out in a minute."

I grabbed a case of beer and hurried out of the storeroom, calling over my shoulder, "Don't worry about it. It's just Paul and Marla in front."

Paul looked up at me with a concerned expression as I set the case on the bar. "That guy going to be okay?"

I plastered a casual smile on. "He'll have a hangover in the morning."

"What'd you do with him?" Marla asked.

I shrugged and winked. "Oh, you know, same thing I do with all the drunks. I stashed him in a hole in the wall to sleep it off."

The concern faded from Paul's and Marla's expressions, and they smiled. "Oh, good," said Marla. "He'll be alright then."

I had always been a storyteller and could invent a lie without the slightest hesitation, but in my experience the best lies were truths told with an ironic smile. It was a skill that had saved my own life, and a few others.

The front door opened and Nick Pieretti walked in looking tired. He clapped Paul on the shoulder and took Marla's extended hand in a friendly greeting before dropping onto a barstool in front of me.

"Long day?" I asked, slipping behind the bar.

"A cop day in Baltimore is the equivalent of three regular person days," he said.

"What can I get you?" I asked. Nick was a police officer who worked out of the Central station. He came in almost every day after work and his answer to that question was always the same, but I still asked.

"Surprise me," he said.

I poured a shot of white rum, then added the cucumber, lime, and mint simple syrup mix I'd made for mojitos, and slid it across the bar. "Anything good happen?"

Nick raised the glass and looked at it with a quirk of his mouth. "I just got dinner in a glass. Cheers." He took a sip and smiled at the flavor. "Nice."

"If that's the only thing green you're getting in your diet, you need a new diet," I said, returning his smile.

Nick was a good-looking guy, but long hours and lots of take-out were leaving a mark.

"Or a new job. Got any openings here?" He asked the question every time he came in. Nick had never been very subtle about his interest in me, and he always took it well when I shot him down.

"Sorry, I've got nothing for you," I responded, then changed the subject like I did every time. "What's been keeping you up too late?"

He sighed and sipped his mojito. Nick was the only guy I knew who admitted he liked fruity drinks, so I tested my recipes on him before I served them to other customers. "Honestly, it's the fear," he shrugged. "The city's full of it. The force is full of it. Everyone's afraid of something or someone, and it's killing all the fun in the job."

"Being a cop is fun?" I asked, intrigued that he'd managed to surprise me.

His smile wiped away the exhaustion in his eyes. "On a good day, it's great. There's a group of kids who play ball over at Patterson. When they let me in on their games, it means everyone made it to school that day and they're not afraid the cop will bust them. And the old guys who play chess in the park have all the stories about the city back in their day – even better when Malcolm's wife sends him with cookies, because he saves me one for when I swing by to check on what they've seen. And you know the Chinese restaurant on Chester? Mrs. Ling uses me as her taster for every new dish she puts on the menu."

"So you're saying the perks are nice," I chuckled. Nick's ease and friendliness were infectious, and he inspired smiles every time he walked into the bar.

"I'll save you half a cookie next time and you'll understand," he grinned. "Actually, why don't you come with me to Ling's? You can try the barbecued duck for yourself."

I smiled and avoided his eyes. "I don't date customers, Nick."

"You eat though, don't you?"

I looked up and met his friendly gaze. "Nope, I don't do that either," I said with a shake of my head.

He groaned and finished his drink, then put a twenty on the bar as he stood to leave.

"The drink's on me tonight." I pushed the money back at him.

"Turns out I don't drink here anymore, which means I'm not a customer you won't date. So consider this the tip on all those drinks I won't be having." He winked and sauntered toward the door. He turned just before he left. "By the way, keep an eye out for a drunk in a black suit. He was in Fells Point about an hour ago – caught on the security system in a pawn shop a couple blocks away. The owner is about one trespasser away from going on a neighborhood rampage."

"You warning me about the drunk or the pawn shop owner?" I asked as casually as I could manage through a frozen smile.

"Both? Just take care, Ren," he said on his way out.

I looked quickly over at Paul and Marla to see if they'd heard Nick's parting shot. They seemed to be deep in conversation, so maybe they hadn't, but I flinched when Macey came in tying a bar apron around her waist. She noticed. "What's wrong? Was that Nick? Did he ask you out again?"

"Watch the bar for a bit, will you, Mace?" I didn't wait for her answer and went straight into the back room. I leaned against the wall and listened as the front door opened and a group of three or four people came in laughing. Good. Macey would be busy behind the bar for a bit.

I shut the door quietly behind me, then pulled the rack out of the way and pushed into the nest. There was Poe, lying exactly where I'd left him on the ground. The drunk in a black suit? Possibly.

I peered at his face, wondering what someone would see on the security cam footage. The mustache was the obvious identifier, and with the longish hair, he could be straight out of the 1970s. I peered closer, wondering if he'd be recognizable without the mustache, and noticed bruises on his jaw and at his temple. They hadn't yet faded to yellows and greens, so they'd happened within the past few days. I debated checking for other damage, but his breathing was still regular and he hadn't vomited yet, so I decided it wasn't completely irresponsible to let him sleep it off.

I did loosen the tie at his neck and unbutton his coat. Something crackled in the pocket, and I slid my hand into it to withdraw three brightly colored slips that appeared to be ballots for an election. They were dated October third with no year, but three ballots didn't end up in a nineteenth-century man's pocket unless he'd been cooped.

I had never encountered the cooping gangs that had run the voting fraud rings in Baltimore, because I couldn't vote back then, but I'd heard about the thugs who kidnapped white men, beat them, plied them with drink and drugs, stuffed their pockets with voting tickets for their candidate, and then on election day took them around to every polling place they could until the men were finally recognized and had to stop voting.

Perhaps Poe had escaped from a coop? It might explain the drunkenness, the bruises, and the ballots. But did it explain the time travel? Beyond the fact that I knew it was possible, time travel was well outside my personal experience. If it *had* been Poe captured on the security cam in a pawn shop, was that where he'd come through? My focus was shifting from the shock of his presence to the problem of what to do with him, but until he woke up, I didn't have enough information to solve it.

I left the ballots on a shelf of the bookcase that dominated one end of the room and quietly pulled the door shut behind me. I locked it, in case Poe woke up and in his stupor came stumbling out, then replaced the rack. I took a deep breath, grabbed a bottle of good cognac, and stepped out into my bar.

Sundays were generally slow nights, so I was able to steer a couple of conversations toward the newest bond measure for school facilities repair and away from talk about the latest crime stats in Fells Point. I had learned long ago that there were things I could impact and things I couldn't. There were wars to fight, battles to win, and arguments to make, and inevitably, I had the best luck with planting the small-scale inception of ideas for change rather than doing anything that would put my face in the news. Standing out front just put the focus on me instead of the issue, and it had never gone well for me when I came out from behind the curtain.

I was able to look in on Poe enough times over the course of the evening to feel certain he wasn't in danger. After I sent Macey home with a take-out container of soup I ordered from the deli next door – they needed the business, and her son had the flu – and made a couple of sandwiches for George, the homeless guy who watched my back door, I went in one last time to check on him before going up to my living quarters above the bar.

Poe no longer looked unconscious. He had moved and was snoring, but he didn't wake when I opened the door to the nest. I wouldn't be up again for hours, so I left a sandwich wrapped in wax paper, a jug of water, and a note on the small table by the door, under which was a chamber pot that had been there forever. Then I locked the door and pushed the rack back into place in front of it. There was plenty to read on the shelves in the nest, though if Poe woke before I returned, he might decide the books weren't enough reason to stay. Hopefully my note would deter him from raising a ruckus or tearing the room apart to find a way out.

I was tired, but my brain was spinning, and as I lay in my bed staring up at the low ceiling of the attic space above the bar, I thought about Edgar Allan Poe. I'd read *The Raven* when it was published, of course. Everyone had. Not many black women of my station could read then, but my mother had been adamant that I learn. *Words are the lights on the path to freedom,* she'd said, as she taught me everything she had learned from my father. I'd started with the Bible and then expanded into newspaper articles and political treatises, pamphlets, and satirical opinions. The day I laid hands on my first novel was the day the world opened for me, and Baltimore became the place my body lived while my mind wandered freely.

Poe's work had figured into my mental landscape, but I had rarely dwelled there. His preoccupation with death was a bit too self-indulgent for my taste. It had always seemed like the height of privilege to worry so much about death, because it implied a right to life which, in my experience, had not been granted.

I didn't have to see the sun to feel it peek above the horizon, and as my body stilled, the last thought I had before my mind quieted was that I hoped Poe was a Descendant of Time so that he could return himself to his native era. Otherwise, I'd have to go in search of a Clocker.

CHAPTER TWO

As always, my first instinct upon waking was to listen – eyes closed, mind clearing of its sleep befuddlement, and senses tuned to the sounds around me. The room where I usually slept was insulated from the street traffic below by thick walls and double-paned glass behind heavy drapes. The old wood in my Colonial Era building still creaked and cracked when someone walked up the stairs or across the floor on the second and third stories, but it had long since settled into silent watchfulness as time marched on outside its brick walls.

I heard nothing, but I was two floors above the secret room where Edgar Allan Poe was, or maybe was not, still sleeping. I jumped up and threw on my uniform of jeans and a man's linen shirt untucked like a tunic. It was still warm enough for flip-flops, and my greenish-gold pedicure was all the embellishment I wore.

I pulled my hair down from the silk scrunchie I wore it in to sleep, pieced the curls apart, and ten minutes later I was on my way down the stairs.

I skipped the sitting room and library on the second floor and went straight down to the hallway that led to the storeroom and bar. The storeroom hadn't been disturbed, and only the dim light from the fading sun illuminated the empty bar beyond.

I turned on the storeroom light and pulled the rack away from the wall, then unlocked the door.

"Mr. Poe?" I spoke just above a whisper. I didn't want to startle him into violence if he was awake, especially since he seemed to have experienced some before he arrived in my bar.

I pushed the door open slowly, giving him time to see me as unthreatening. "Mr. Poe, are you awake?"

The light in the nest was still on, and I could see that the sandwich and water had been moved off the small table. "My name is Ren – Alexandra Reynolds. You've been hurt, but you're safe here," I said quietly. "The door was closed to protect you, but you're free to come out if you'd like."

There was still no movement from the nest. I knew what it felt like to be cornered, and realized that even weak from a hangover, Poe was likely strong enough to do damage to me if he was afraid. So I backed up, turned a chair around, and straddled it so I faced the door to the secret room from about six feet away.

I leaned forward, resting my arms on the chair back, and considered Poe's condition. If he had, indeed, escaped a cooping situation, then he'd most likely been drugged, starved, and beaten. "I have more food if you'd like," I said softly. Everything in the storeroom was alcoholic, but I kept basic food supplies in the refrigerator behind the bar so I could feed George and anyone who wandered in The Door hungry.

I thought I heard him shuffle his position slightly, but he still didn't emerge from the nest, so I remained where I was. I debated singing something he would recognize but decided against it, as I didn't particularly love the songs from that time. Then I considered what I knew of Poe's work, and the tune to an Appalachian folk version of *Annabel Lee* came into my head. I must have begun to hum, because I was aware that the music died away when Poe finally stepped into the open doorway.

He looked pale and shaky, as one does with the mother of all hangovers, and it was obvious he'd finally vomited at some point during the day because it was matted in his mustache and stained his shirt and coat. He winced as his gaze swept over the cases and bottles of liquor stacked in the storeroom, and when he studied me, I looked back steadily.

"Where is your master?" he finally said.

I held my casual pose as I continued to meet his eyes. "I am my own master." My blood pulsed with an anger I'd thought long buried, but I kept my tone neutral.

"The owner of this establishment then," he said with a hint of impatience.

"You're looking at her," I answered as I stood and pushed the chair away. "I'll show you to the bathroom, and you can wash while I find you something else to wear."

He gave me a critical once-over. "'Tis not I who requires a change of clothing."

I gave him the same up-and-down gaze, landing on the vomit stains with a raised eyebrow. He looked down at himself and scowled.

"Where is my satchel?" He sounded accusing.

"You arrived empty-handed," I said. Poe remained still, as though he'd taken root, and I saw anger and fear at war in his expression.

"You are a stranger here, sir," I said carefully. "You stumbled in my door, bruised and drunk, carrying nothing but ballots in your pockets that I assume were given to you by roughskins. I offer you a place to clean yourself, something to wear, a meal, and a quiet place to determine what happened to you and what to do next."

He narrowed his eyes at me. "You say I am a stranger here, yet you know my name."

"As does anyone who has read your work."

"I find it unlikely you know how to read," he scoffed.

I crossed my arms in front of my chest and glared.

"*Once upon a midnight dreary, while I pondered, weak and weary,*
Over many a quaint and curious volume of forgotten lore,
While I nodded, nearly napping, suddenly there came a tapping,
As of some one gently rapping, rapping at my chamber door.
'Tis some visitor,' I muttered, 'tapping at my chamber door —
Only this, and nothing more.'"

The look of startled amazement on his face gave me a small bit of satisfaction, but I was still irritated. "As likely as you are to be a thorn in my side, no one deserves the treatment you apparently received at the hands of an election gang. You are in some trouble, and I will do what I can to help."

I turned and left the storeroom before he could say anything else, and I was out at the bar, closed on Monday nights, fixing a plate of cheese, crackers, and grapes when he found me. He looked around the room, which I'd designed in warm tones of orange and burnished gold. I redecorated every time I came back to Baltimore, but The Door had worn these colors for almost ten years. It was nearly time for me to find a place to go for new inspiration.

"I assume," Poe began cautiously, "that you have no husband and are perhaps a madam or procuress. If so, might I inquire as to the nature of your custom so that I might find a man who can help me?"

It took me exactly one second to translate the question. "You see a black woman of independent means and assume that the only way I could earn such luxuries is on my back?"

"It is not an unreasonable assumption." He scowled back at me.

I stared at him as I forcibly reminded myself of the world as he knew it, and I decided I wasn't going to meet his expectations just to make him more comfortable. "It's not only unreasonable, it's insulting."

There was a moment of shock before he scowled again and looked me up and down with an expression that was dangerously close to contempt. "Your race and your sex are clear for any to see. If you own this establishment, what else should I assume? What other business can someone like you engage in?"

Someone like me. It had been years since anyone had been overtly degrading toward me in my own place, and I found myself warming to the fight with a long-suppressed anger and years of higher education in my back pocket. "As I said, you are a stranger here, and here, no human being is born less than any other. None. My sex, as you call it, comprises more than half of the world's population, and white and black people account for approximately equal slices in a pie chart of world ethnicities. Together, our races make up barely one-fourth of the total, so demographically speaking, our numbers and relative influence are the same."

He stared at me. "A pie chart of world ethnicities?"

The dried vomit in his mustache was making me twitchy, and the conversation needed a change of subject before I said something I'd regret.

"You stink, and there's vomit on your suit. You can use the shower upstairs to clean up, if you can tolerate using the same bathroom I do."

I stepped out from behind the bar and went down the hall and up the staircase to the second floor. I had locked both front and back doors, so even if he wanted to leave the building, he couldn't, which meant he'd either drink everything in my bar or he would follow me upstairs.

The sound of feet striding down the hall toward the back door made me tired. I was going to have to keep him locked in when I slept so he didn't escape into twenty-first century Baltimore. I hated locking people in. Locking them out was so much simpler.

CHAPTER THREE

My favorite room in the building – the largest and most comfortable – was my library. I had amassed a huge collection of books in my lifetime, some of which had become quite valuable and all of which I'd read. There was a round table near a window where I worked, a comfortable chair for reading, and a long sofa for stretching out. I walked in and turned on a table lamp, then opened another door that led to a second bedroom that I'd turned into a large bathroom. After a few moments, I heard Poe on the staircase.

"You have no right to hold me prisoner," he said angrily. But then his breath caught, and I turned to see what had surprised him. Edgar Allan Poe stood in the doorway to my library staring in awe at the shelves full of books. His mouth hung open as his eyes searched the floor-to-ceiling bookcases with the sort of intensity one usually reserved for decoding a cipher.

"These are your books?" he breathed.

"Yes," I said without elaboration.

He stepped forward and held a hand out as if to touch the gilt spines of the Shakespeare plays, but then saw the spot of dried vomit on his sleeve and pulled back with a wince. "I believe I would like to wash myself if you would show me where I might have use of a bucket or a tub."

He met my eyes briefly, but then looked away, as if he were loath to ask.

"Come." I led him into the bathroom and turned on the light. Poe gasped as he looked up at the chandelier I'd found on Craigslist.

"What is this lamp that illuminates as though by magic?"

I'd rewired it myself, so I actually could answer that question, but instead I busied myself with the tub. I plugged the drain of the big cast iron tub that I'd positioned in the middle of the wood floor, then turned on the hot water to let it fill. "The lights, the plumbing – all of this will require a longer conversation that I promise to have with you, but not yet. Bathe first, and then we'll talk while you eat."

I made sure the water temperature was right, then took a big white towel out of the cabinet. "I'll be right back with some clothes," I said. Poe had turned his stunned gaze from the lights to the running bath when I slipped out past him.

I took the stairs two at a time up to my bedroom and grabbed a linen shirt similar to the one I wore, a pair of loose sweatpants, and a clean pair of socks. I hadn't paid attention to Poe's footwear, but thought he might have boots.

The door to the bathroom remained open, and Poe was still staring at the rising water with fascination when I entered. "Here are clean clothes – you can leave yours in here when you're done." I set the clothes on the counter, went over and cranked off the water faucet, then met Poe's startled gaze.

"Take as long as you like, and then pull the drain plug when you're finished."

As I was closing the door behind me, I heard his quiet voice. "Thank you, Mistress Ren."

I was deeply engrossed in my fourth re-read of *The Code Book* when Poe silently padded into the room. He smelled faintly of soap and looked somehow younger, even in his slightly ridiculous outfit of a shirt buttoned to the chin and tucked into sweatpants. His hair was wet and had been finger-combed into a semblance of order, and his fingertips were pale and shriveled from the long soak.

His gaze once again swept the bookshelves. He seemed reluctant to sit.

"You're welcome to read anything you find on the shelves," I said.

He darted a quick glance at me. "How did you acquire such a library?"

"I've collected books through the years. It's easy enough to do when one keeps the same address for as long as I have." I knew that I looked to be in my early thirties, so his reference for 'long' would be different than mine. I closed my book and switched subjects. "The food is for you, and I can make coffee or tea, whichever you prefer."

Again he looked startled, as though surprised at my offer. "Tea, please. Thank you."

I got up and went into the small butler's pantry where I kept an electric tea kettle and different varieties of tea. I'd long ago gotten out of the habit of guests, but "just in case" was a phrase I'd never lost. I didn't bother to ask which kind he preferred, since variety was likely not something he was used to.

He was standing at the shelves reading the spines of books in the mystery section when I returned with his tea. I reclaimed my seat in the reading chair and watched as Poe pulled a 1941 Limited Editions Club hard copy of *TALES of Mystery & Imagination by E.A. POE* from the shelf. The spine was embossed with gold ink, and the front and back boards were covered in a swirled blue, red, orange, and white pattern. He touched the cover reverently but pushed it back into place without opening it. I sighed in relief. It had been years since I'd read that volume, but I seemed to remember a long-winded biography of Poe at the beginning, which would undoubtedly have been disturbing for him to read. I didn't remember the details and was abruptly glad it wasn't fresh in my mind. That he was dead, I already knew. When and how he died was too much information to have about a man who stood right in front of me.

I waited for his first question.

He moved to the sofa to sit, and when he picked up his tea mug, he finally marshalled his thoughts to speak. "It is clear to me, Mistress Ren, that you are a lady of quality. I apologize for any offense I may have given earlier."

"You were offensive, and I forgive you," I said.

My candor seemed to surprise him. "I find I am at a loss for what to say, for everything I consider seems, on second thought, to be too personal or indecorous, and my questions would serve only to display my marked ignorance about the situation in which I now find myself."

I exhaled. "Your ignorance is not just about your situation, but I will be patient with your ignorance and try not to take offense at things you don't have the experience to see differently."

His expression was inscrutable, and he seemed to think for a long time about what to say next. "Where am I?" he finally asked.

"You're in Fells Point, Baltimore. My bar is called The Door, and I own this building," I said.

"How?" His eyes narrowed at me, and I realized we were back to the small questions about my ability to own anything. Well, I wasn't having it.

"*When* is the question you should be asking," I said sternly. "*When* are you?"

That got his attention, and he stood suddenly and went to the window which overlooked George's shelter in the back alley behind my building. There was nothing particularly anachronistic to see out there though, so I held out the book I'd been reading. "I read this for the first time about a decade ago. It wasn't a new book then."

He opened *The Code Book* to the copyright page to read the original publication date. His eyes widened as he closed the cover, looked at the title, then opened it again. "When am I?" he finally asked in an awed whisper.

"You've Clocked to the twenty-first century," I said, watching him carefully.

He seemed to falter. "I … I've clocked?"

Oh no, my mind whispered, *please no*. "You *are* a Clocker, aren't you?"

He scowled impatiently. "I am many things, madam, but I do not count clock-maker among my professions."

I sighed and indicated that he should sit back down on the couch. "Settle in, Poe. Eat something. This is going to require a suspension of disbelief."

He obeyed me, warily, and picked up his mug of tea again.

"Have you ever found yourself in an unfamiliar place with no idea how you got there? Or maybe it was a place you recognized, but everything else felt … off?"

He seemed to relax fractionally, and then nodded. "Fever dreams," he said simply.

"Fever dreams?"

Then he looked somewhat sheepish, and it was such a strange expression on his pompous face that I almost laughed. I managed to control the impulse, and he explained. "Very occasionally, when the muse has been silent for too long, a bout of melancholia will strike me down and I'll take to my bed, a strong libation being the only cure for the sleeplessness that ensues."

"So," I translated, "you drink yourself into a stupor when you get writer's block."

He scowled at me, but I kept a straight face as if I hadn't enjoyed the dig.

"Indeed," he said. "The fever dreams from those stupors …?" I nodded, and he continued, "They have resulted in the genesis of some of my more inspired works."

Poe had time traveled and seen or heard about things he incorporated into his stories? It would be easy enough to check. "For example?" I prompted.

"Well," he took a sip of his tea, "I wrote *The Narrative of Arthur Gordon Pym* after one such incident. The scene with Richard Parker was particularly vivid in my imagination."

I made a mental note to look up Richard Parker.

"And *The Business Man* came to me quite readily after another such stupor, as you call it," he added. His eyes had wandered back to the bookshelves behind me. "And I once dreamed that I read a book about the formation of the universe …" – he seemed to shake himself back to awareness – "But nothing of that could have anything to do with what has happened to me now, surely."

I shrugged. "I have no idea. It's possible you're a Clocker and you've never known how you do it. The fact that you're drunk each time doesn't help, because I don't know how the Descendants of

Time use portals to time travel, beyond the fact that they do, and I was hoping you'd know how it works."

"The Descendants of Time?" he asked. "Portals?"

I considered Poe for a long moment. I'd already told him far more than was wise for a man with his imagination to know and possibly write about when he returned to his native time. "What's the last thing you remember before you woke up here?"

If the abrupt change of subject confused him, he rolled with it gracefully. "I remember departing Richmond for Philadelphia, and … that is all." He suddenly looked confused, as if the erasure of his memory had never happened before.

"Do you remember arriving here in my bar last night?"

He shook his head. "I do not."

I sighed. "I think you may have been caught by a cooping gang in Baltimore. I found multiple ballots in your pocket, and the bruises on your face would indicate you've been beaten. What year was it when you left Richmond?"

He looked surprised. "It was 1849, of course."

"Right," I said. I pulled my phone out of my pocket, ignored Poe's startled gaze, and searched October 3, 1849. The first results came up, and I felt the blood drain from my face as I read the words, *Mysterious death of Edgar A. Poe.* I quickly shut down the phone and tucked it back into my pocket. Bad enough that he'd seen me do something inexplicable, worse to know what I'd found.

The buzzer sounded from downstairs. It was the back door buzzer – the only door I would answer when the bar was closed. I unfurled myself from the chair.

"Check the publication dates on more books if you need to prove to yourself that you are no longer in 1849, but please stay here while I see who's here so late. I would not like to have to explain your presence."

CHAPTER FOUR

I ran down the stairs, checking the camera app on my phone as I did. It was Nick Pieretti. Off duty, by the state of his dress, but still a cop.

I unlocked and opened the heavy back door. "Nick."

"Can I come in?"

"Why?"

"Please?" he said.

"I'm busy."

He sighed. "Just for a minute. Please, Ren."

I considered him for a moment. I liked Nick and I'd never been intentionally rude to him. Now was not the time to behave in a way that was out of character. I stepped back from the door and let him into the hall, then led him through the building to the bar. The running lights were the only illumination in the big room, and I left it that way. I directed him to a table, where I pulled out a chair and sat. He dropped into a seat across from me and looked around the dimly lit room.

"You got any ghosts in the place?"

I held back a shiver at his prescience. "Why are you here, Nick?"

"I want to get to know you. I've been coming in The Door for two years, and the only conversations we ever have are about three minutes long if I happen to grab a barstool right in front of the register."

"I've told you, I don't date customers," I said quietly.

"And I'm sitting here, across the table from you in a closed bar, clearly not a customer. I will back off if you're genuinely not interested, but I'd like to hope you wouldn't make that call without getting to know me first."

I scoffed. "What if I were gay, Nick? Would that be an acceptable reason not to date you?"

"Maybe. Probably." He looked chagrinned. "Are you?"

I bit back the smile that threatened. "Not particularly."

"Not …" he sat back with a mischievous grin, "not particularly?"

"Nick, I'm not going to play mental fantasy games with you. I'm not playing any games with you. I do not date. Period."

The smile dropped from his face and he leaned forward, resting his arms on the table. "Are you married?"

I scowled but didn't answer.

"I mean, I don't think you're married. I wouldn't do that – pursue a married woman. That's not cool."

I got up from the table. "I have things to do."

His expression fell into something that looked defeated as he stood to follow me out of the bar and back down the hall. "I'm sorry, Ren. I just really hoped that if you got to know me a little outside our usual cop/bartender roles, you might let yourself like me."

"I do like you, Nick," I said, facing him as I opened the door. "You're funny, and charming, and—"

"Handsome?" he supplied hopefully.

I laughed. "You know you're handsome. But my life is complicated, and I don't make that anyone else's problem." He was standing too close in the small hallway, and I wanted to push him out the back door.

"But who do you get hugs from, Ren?" he said quietly as he looked down into my eyes.

My breath stuttered and then caught, and slowly – so slowly I could easily duck away if I wanted to – Nick put his arms around me and pulled me close to his chest.

I was enveloped in his arms, and the only motion I could feel was the beating of his heart beneath my ear and the pounding of mine throughout my body. He held me, so warm, so alive, so human, and I let myself sink into him for one breathtaking moment, until the scent of his skin and the flutter of his pulse brought me back to myself, and I pulled away.

"Good night, Nick," I whispered, unable to meet his eyes.

I could feel his gaze searching my face as I looked past him through the open door into the cooling night air.

He cleared his throat, as if to get his voice back to normal volume. "Lock your doors, okay? We haven't caught the drunk yet, but CCTV put him right around here."

"The drunk?" I dragged my gaze back to his face.

"The one they found in the pawn shop. We have the security cam footage up on the news to try to get him turned in. He must have really scared the owner, and now the guy is out for blood."

I nodded quickly. "Yeah, I'll lock the door."

He looked like he wanted to say something else, but then shook his head and walked out. I watched him head down the alley, and then I locked the door quietly behind him.

I exhaled, and leaned back against the wall. Why? Why did Nick have to make it personal, to reach past all my carefully constructed social distancing measures into the one fissure in my defenses – human touch. It had been so long …

I missed hugs.

The floor above me creaked, and I realized I'd lived alone so many years that it was a shock to hear someone moving around my building. Nick said the police had made the security cam footage public, and I needed to know if it was Poe in that pawn shop so I could figure out what to do with the guy in the room above my head. I pulled my phone out of my back pocket and navigated to the Baltimore PD Twitter feed, then scrolled down to the black-and-white footage in the WANTED post.

It was grainy and eerie in the way infrared footage is in dim light, but the man stumbling away from the wall toward the staircase was definitely Edgar Allan Poe. The room was full of all the things I expected to see in the cellar of a pawn shop, plus one drunk human no one would ever think to see in the twenty-first century.

I sighed and kicked off the wall.

I considered my options as I climbed the staircase. This didn't have to be my problem. Just because Edgar Allan Poe had stumbled into my bar didn't mean he was my responsibility.

I groaned. Who was I kidding? Even when things ended spectacularly badly, as they certainly had before, *anyone* who stumbled into my place was my responsibility. It was how I'd always been and probably always would be. It just happened less often now than it used to, most likely because no one really remembered I was here.

I'd worked hard on my invisibility skills, but that meant I didn't know of any Immortal Descendants living in the greater Baltimore area. It's not like there was a hotline to call when someone needed a Clocker portal. The few hints I had about Descendants came from whispered conversations when I was a child and a memorable encounter when I was a young woman. Since then, I had run into very few Descendants of the five Families in Baltimore, though among them had been the Seer who sat at my bar during Prohibition one night drinking tea laced with whiskey from his own flask, telling me everything he Saw about the patrons around us.

By the time the flask was empty, the Seer had informed me that I was not normal. The Family I belonged to, he'd said, was made up of loners, outcasts, and travelers who never put down roots or lived in communities of any kind for longer than a few years. The fact that I'd been in Baltimore most of my life had stunned and him, and he had considered sticking around, just to see how things turned out for me.

He didn't survive the winter.

Self-isolation meant that I had no easy access to other Descendants, and basic humanity meant I had no will to kick Poe out into a time that wasn't his own. The only option I saw was to figure out how he'd managed to Clock himself here and get him to do it again in reverse.

Poe was seated on the couch, engrossed in my book. He sat primly, with back straight and his legs crossed at the thigh. His posture forcibly reminded me of the comportment lessons my grandmother had given me. How I'd hated all the rules, until Grandmother Alexandra had explained that they were her means of survival as a woman in a society that did not value a woman's mind, her heart, or her will. *The best camouflage for living outside the rules is to hide behind them*, she'd said. I wondered if she had known how prophetic her words would be to a woman who had survived precisely because of that camouflage.

I crossed the room and sat in my chair, my legs curled under me in deliberate defiance of my grandmother's rules. "You came here through a portal of some kind — a door of sorts that only opens for certain people. You seem to be one of those people."

Poe looked up from my book. "A door that is a door only for one able to open it." He frowned. "Presumably, the action that brought me here could be done in reverse?"

"That's usually how it works," I said, "but I'm not a Clocker, so I don't know what a portal looks like, and apparently, neither do you."

"And yet I can open one." Poe considered this for a long moment as he turned *The Code Book* over in his hands. "Perhaps," he finally said, "I know more than I realize. How well do you understand secret codes?"

"I've read that book several times, and I've used encryption myself in situations where it was warranted. Why do you ask?"

"Encryption?" He pondered the word, and I realized I didn't exactly know when it had come into popular use. "From *kruptos,* perhaps? The Greek word for hidden." His gaze returned to me. "In any case, I confess that I find it entirely fascinating that the meaning of one thing can be hidden inside something entirely different, but that in order to unlock that meaning, the key must be accessible to the one for whom the message is intended."

"Like deciphering your poetry, for example."

He smiled slowly, as if the desire to smile was a surprise. "It is true that I bury meanings beneath words of a different cast in much of my poetry. I enjoy challenging my readers to stretch beyond what they know into what they could possibly imagine."

"How does that help us find a portal to get you home?"

"You accused me of being a 'Clocker.' It is a term with which I am unfamiliar, except, of course, in the purely mechanical sense. And yet, upon closer rumination, it seems that I am intimately familiar with clocks and their imagery, as they appear throughout my work in what I now perceive to be very intriguing ways."

I leaned forward. "*The Pit and the Pendulum*."

"That is not even the most evocative clock image, but yes, of course," he said with an air of satisfaction. "In addition to *The Man of the Crowd*, *William Wilson*, *The Devil in the Belfry*, *A Predicament*, and, of course, *The Masque of the Red Death*."

I considered what I knew of his work. I hadn't read all of the stories he'd named, but barring a literary deconstruction, I couldn't see any common thread beyond the clock imagery.

My words were carefully measured. "If we operate under the assumption that your subconscious mind was encoding a message within your work, how would you interpret your use of clocks in your stories?"

He looked thoughtful. "My subconscious mind? Sub, meaning beneath, and conscious, from the Latin *conscius*, or knowing." His gaze met mine as he stood and returned *The Code Book* to the small table near my chair. "Mistress Ren, I find your grasp of the question to be extraordinary. One might assume you were a man for the clear, concise way you see past the information given to that which lies beneath."

I smirked. "I appreciate that you believe you are complimenting me, Poe, so I'll take the compliment in the spirit in which it was meant."

He slanted a look at me that could have been interpreted as impatient. I ignored it as he continued to pace the room.

"Perhaps less important than what clocks signify is the form and shape they take, if, indeed, we seek to find the portal through which I have traveled."

I nodded. "That's pretty brilliant, actually. Find the common themes for the clocks, and maybe the form is hidden among them." I got up and retrieved a notebook and pencil from a drawer in the table, then returned to my chair and looked at him expectantly.

"So, where should we begin?"

CHAPTER FIVE

We worked our way through everything he'd ever written that included a clock. Our search produced pendulums, clock hands, staircases, and keyholes. Of these, the most likely to have been associated with a portal that Poe could reasonably access were spiral staircases, keyholes, and of course, the clocks themselves.

The pawn shop where Poe had come into this time had to have a portal in or near it. I needed to find the address and determine whether it would be possible to get him back in there at a time when the place was closed.

I pulled out my phone and found the pawn shop video. Poe sat on the sofa reading *The Code Book* while I replayed the image of him on the small screen stumbling forward into frame and then away toward the stairs. The image held on the empty frame for a moment longer before it clipped out. Nothing in the footage specifically identified the name of the business, so I did an internet search for 'pawn shop,' 'Baltimore,' and 'drunk.' Remarkably, I got a hit from a local news station whose reporter interviewed the pawn shop owner about the incident. The owner was vitriolic in his anger against the homeless, the drunks, and the drug dealers who had taken over the streets, and unfortunately, I knew him.

"The bad guys are winning right now. It's going to be up to the good guys to keep ourselves safe," he snarled to the camera before the news report cut back to the anchor at the desk.

"Great," I murmured. The guy was a regular in the bar. His pawn shop was three blocks over from my building next to some Colonial Era row houses.

"I'm going out," I announced as I unpeeled myself from the chair. "I want to check out a possible location for your portal."

Poe set the book aside. "I'll come with you."

"No," I said abruptly.

He flinched. "I have given you the courtesy of listening to your words, but you go too far in thinking to command me. I will not be told no."

I just barely refrained from the scoff that statement deserved. "You'll not only be told no, you'll respect the no. You don't belong in this time, you don't understand it, and if someone recognizes you, there could be trouble."

"Surely the street isn't safe for a woman alone at night," he scowled.

"Nor is it safe for many men. Nor," I glared at him, "was it safe for you when you arrived in Baltimore in your own time and were captured by a cooping gang. I thank you for your concern, but

I'll be fine. Just please stay inside the building while I'm gone." I looked steadily at him, and finally he averted his eyes.

"It offends me to have a woman conduct my business for me."

"Funny," I said, with a raised eyebrow, "it offends me to have a bigot in my house. Here's hoping we both find tolerance."

I sprinted upstairs and quickly changed into running gear. I preferred to do my workouts either right after sunset or just before dawn, but running would at least give me an excuse to be out by myself.

When I returned to the library, Poe stood at the window that looked down on the back alley. "Someone is sleeping down there," he said simply.

"That's George. He's homeless. I feed him and he keeps an eye on things."

Poe turned to face me. "How is it that there are such things as lights that require no fire, and yet the streets are still not safe and there remain those without a home?"

The question startled me. Actually, it wasn't the question itself that startled me – it was one I'd considered often, as it had been debated and discussed by all people in every era through which I'd lived. But I'd actually read some of Poe's favorable reviews of pro-slavery books when he edited *The Southern Literary Messenger*, and I was startled that a man with his sympathies had done the asking.

I chose my words carefully. "There is an assumption by many that rewards will go to those who earn them; that without effort, poverty or homelessness is deserved." He nodded, whether in agreement or acknowledgement, I wasn't sure. "That way of thinking assumes a level playing field, where no advantages of education, opportunity, health, or circumstance exist."

I looked Poe directly in the eyes. "Consider a person who was enslaved in your time – property in the eyes of your law. That person's descendants are now free and equal in the eyes of mine. Will the playing field between the enslaved person's descendants and the master's ever be equal? And if so, how many generations will that take?"

Poe opened his mouth to speak, but I wasn't done. "What about you, an artist who was barely paid a subsistence wage for your work when you produced it, and yet that same work has continued to be read by people for nearly six generations?" I nodded to the volume of his work he'd found earlier. "Imagine if your life had been subsidized, either by your family or by the government. How many more works of literary art might you have been able to produce if you weren't terrified your family wouldn't eat?"

I took a deep breath and steered my own response back to the question he'd asked. "The answer to your question is that there's no simple answer, and you're right, innovation has advanced far beyond electricity, and yet we remain unwilling to provide basic living standards to all our citizens."

He considered me for a long moment. "This appears to be a topic about which you are quite passionate."

I exhaled slowly. "It is."

"And yet you live alone in a building that could comfortably house many, including this man, George, whom you feed but do not shelter. I seek not to judge your choices, merely to understand them."

My expression was granite. "You have no idea how many I have housed and protected and given safe harbor to." I could hear the fury vibrating in my tone, even as my throat was closing with a familiar feeling of helplessness.

"But no matter how many people I saved, there were always so … many more." The anger drained away just as quickly as it had hit, and I swallowed the tears that I'd stopped crying so many years before. There was a time when the buzz of fury was the source of my ability to open my eyes and face every day. But that time had faded, and with each year, the distance between who I'd been and who I'd become seemed greater than just the passage of time.

I inhaled slowly and met Poe's keen gaze. "I have felt passionately about many things in my life. Occasionally, I sat behind my walls, reading and learning and honing my beliefs. There were other times when I spoke out, and times when I stood up, fought, and bled for my beliefs. Invariably, those times ended badly for me or someone I loved." Pain tightened my chest, and I breathed deeply to loosen the familiar feelings of loss.

"Believing in something is easy enough – it is anonymous, and can be done from a distance. But change requires more – it needs voices and faces, people to say the words and do the deeds." I shook my head at the memories of who I'd once been. "I have chosen battles to fight, and there were battles I sat out, even knowing that a fight was needed."

I grabbed my cell phone from the table and stuck it in the pocket of my leggings. "But you're right. There are ways I can make a difference even when I choose to sit out the fight." I looked out the window and considered the night. I knew I'd be thinking about Poe's words long after he'd gone, even as I resisted the pain that went along with them. "I'm going for a run – I'll see you in about an hour."

I left him there, with the books and whatever thoughts he might have about my outburst. But when I locked the back door behind me, I took a moment to scan the alley for George. There was no movement from his little shelter, so he was either asleep or out wandering the city. I resolved that the next time I saw him, I would invite him in to use the bar's bathroom and to eat at a table if he wanted to. And then I wondered how I had let myself get so alone that I hadn't done it before.

CHAPTER SIX

Mike's pawn shop was just a couple of blocks from The Door, and the place gave the whole neighborhood a slightly seedy appearance. I slowed my jog to a walk and noticed the little differences like chains around bicycles and heavy-duty locks on the doors, which were a revealing testament to an elevated level of fear among the inhabitants there. That didn't bode well for Poe's ability to get back into the pawn shop.

Whenever Mike was in my bar, conversation around him inevitably turned to guns, crime, and the people who would be shot if they ever tried to break into his place. There was a surveillance camera mounted above the door and a heavy chain wrapped around the double door handles closed tightly with a large padlock. The chain looked new, and I wondered if it had been added because of Poe. The building was a two-story pre-Civil War brick row house with a full basement, and when I saw a curtain twitch in a window overlooking the street, I thought it was likely that Mike lived upstairs, so I continued my run down the block, past other row houses toward the patch of greenery at the end. I still needed to exercise, and the night air was crisp and carried the scent of rain.

I changed my usual route and traveled streets I hadn't been on in years. The historic districts remained my favorite parts of Baltimore, but new construction had gone up everywhere. I let my feet take me wherever my eyes led, and I marveled at the details. For years I'd blended into the background noise of the city, not allowing myself to dwell in the foreground of anything. I'd made sure no photos had been taken of me since I'd come back to The Door a decade before, so no images existed for comparison as time passed. In a world where snapshots of people's lives were almost more real than the lives themselves, I had ceased to exist. Only the person who sat at my bar knew my face, and when those people saw me day after day, they stopped seeing the details. It was a common human condition to lose sight of the things we saw most often. I'd done it with George, and I wondered what else I had missed.

I turned my focus back to the task at hand, and as my mind wandered through the imagery of Poe's clocks, my gaze danced across the scenery. There were planters full of late-blooming flowers, new window displays in vintage shops, and playful clothing on headless forms. A chandelier sparkled in the bay window of a dining room, a forgotten ball lay hidden under some steps, and there, on the sidewalk before me, a child's chalk drawing of a spiral filled the sidewalk.

I halted, the images in my mind suddenly clashing with the one on the ground. Poe's clock symbolism had included spirals – lots of them. A long spiral staircase going up to a clock tower in *A Predicament*, the circular motion of the hands of the clock, the dancers and the very shape of the rooms in *The Masque of the Red Death* – all were spirals.

I turned back the way I'd come and pushed myself to run faster than before. Spirals. How many movies and comic books used spirals to indicate time travel? And if it were true that the portal was a spiral, was there another one that could take Poe back to 1849?

The thought of that date carved a hole in my gut that filled with acid. According to the quick search I'd done on the October 3, 1849 election, the most notable thing about that day was that it was when Edgar Allan Poe had been found outside a polling place in Baltimore, apparently drunk and ill. He'd been taken to a hospital and died four days later.

I couldn't scrub the knowledge from my brain, and I didn't know what to do with it. Keep searching for the way to send him back, knowing that if I succeeded, he would die within days of his return, or let him stay here and … then what? Keep him? The idea of being responsible for an out-of-time anti-abolitionist held no appeal to a mixed-race Southern woman with far too much experience with the ideas of his time. And if he didn't go back, what unknown effects could that have on the events in his time? I had to send him back if I could and let fate take over from there.

My footsteps slowed as I approached the pawn shop block again. This time I didn't turn the corner onto the street, but instead darted down the back alley behind the buildings. It was after midnight, and the darkness felt desolate in a way that reminded me of lock-downs and curfews. I didn't like the vulnerability that came with the desolation.

I had just passed the back door of the pawn shop when I felt a shiver of awareness crawl up my spine. Someone was watching me, and my fight-or-flight instinct kicked in hard. I tensed to run when I heard the low voice from the shadows.

"What are you doing here?"

My heart pounded as adrenaline surged through my veins. I turned around slowly, keeping my hands loose and visible at my sides.

"Nick," I breathed, wariness warring with relief. Interested in me or not, Nick Pieretti was still a cop. He took a step forward out of the shadow of the building he'd been leaning against, and I instinctively took a half-step back. I didn't mean to do it, and the instant of suspicion that crossed his face made me wish I hadn't, but I'd lived too long to take my security for granted.

"Why are you here, Ren?" His low voice held a warning.

"Why are you?" I shot back.

He seemed to consider that for a moment and then surprised me by answering. "I walk when I can't sleep."

"I read," I said automatically. It was true. I'd spent very long nights alone with my books.

A smile tugged at the corners of his mouth. "What are you reading?"

"*The Code Book*," I answered truthfully. "About code-making and breaking throughout history. I watched the footage of the drunk guy on the security cam and realized I knew the owner of the pawn shop." I nodded up at the back of the building. "Mike's a customer at The Door. It made me curious about the building, and I wondered how the guy got in."

If he was surprised, he didn't show it. "I've been wondering that too," he said. He indicated the pawn shop. "The owner lives upstairs, so it's not like the guy could have snuck in and hid while he was out. If I hadn't seen the footage myself, I wouldn't have believed it."

"The drunk didn't actually do anything, did he? I mean, there wasn't anything missing or broken?"

Nick shook his head. "Nothing. Honestly, it was like the guy was in the wrong building, realized it, and got the hell out. Apparently the locks were all deadbolts that could be thrown from inside, so the bigger question is how did he get in?"

Interesting, but if I was right, getting Poe in *again* was the bigger issue. "So why are you out here walking off your sleepless night?" I asked.

Nick scoffed. "You're going to think I'm crazy."

I shrugged. "Does it matter what I think?"

He looked sideways at me. "I'd like it to." Then he shook his head. "It sounds nuts even to me, and my tolerance for inexplicable things is off the charts."

That gave me pause. For the two years Nick had been coming into The Door, he'd just seemed like a regular guy's guy – not too deep, not too serious or too curious – just easy with a smile and a flirtatious comment, and generally straightforward in a 'what you see is what you get' kind of way.

"I believe in things I can't explain," I said quietly.

He glanced at me again, then seemed to decide to trust me. "The guy on the security cam – the drunk guy – looks like Edgar Allan Poe."

It didn't even surprise me when he said the words. Having seen the footage, I half-expected someone to make the connection, but I didn't expect it to be Nick Pieretti. "I didn't take you for a reader," I said finally.

Nick scowled at me. "Poe is probably the whole reason mystery novels exist. His suspense writing was way ahead of its time, and you should know, since you're reading a book about ciphers, that he was totally into secret codes. He used one as a main plot point in *The Gold Bug*, and also ran a cryptography contest in one of the magazines he edited, challenging readers to send him ciphers to break. Apparently, he solved them all."

"I didn't know you were so into secret codes, Nick," I said, quelling the smile his enthusiasm almost inspired.

He scoffed. "I dare you to find any kid who wasn't. Some of us just never grew out of it."

"What do you know about clocks in Poe's work?" I asked, not really sure where I was going with the question.

"I know they're all through it," Nick said with a shrug. "Why?"

"Just something I've been working on." I started walking away down the alley toward my own building. Nick fell into step next to me.

"What do you think about what I said – that the drunk looks like Poe?" he asked, almost too casually, as if doing a check on my assessment of his sanity.

"I think you're right, he does. I'm just not sure what that has to do with anything," I said with an equally casual tone.

He sighed. "Me either. It's just weird."

We walked together in silence, and I gradually realized he was matching his stride to mine. "You don't have to walk me home, Nick."

"Unless you have superpowers you haven't told me about, I'm walking you home."

I scoffed with a laugh. "But I do."

"Yeah? Like what?"

I shrugged. "Immortality."

He looked over at me with a grin. "Cool. Is it catching?"

I couldn't help the answering smile. "Could be, but I'm not giving it to you."

His expression fell comically. "Bummer. Well, good to know you can't die. But I'm still going to walk you home so none of the non-fatal things happen to you either."

I chuckled, and we continued past the front of my building around to the alley in back. George was just shuffling in from the other end, and as he reached his small shelter, he tipped an imaginary hat to me as he usually did.

"Do you need to use the bathroom, George?" I asked, startling both Nick and the homeless man, who stared at me in surprise.

"No ma'am. I mean … no, thank you, ma'am." George seemed flustered, and Nick looked at me with a strange expression on his face.

I nodded. "Well, I'll open the back door just before dawn. If you want to use the bathroom then, please come in. I'll leave a towel for you, and a toothbrush and toothpaste. You can keep them under the sink if you'd like."

"Thank you, ma'am. That's most generous of you," George said with another imaginary tip of his hat.

I unlocked my back door and then turned to say goodbye to Nick. He looked bemused. "Thanks for walking me home."

"You're seriously going to invite that guy in to your building?"

I looked him straight in the eyes. "Yes."

He turned to study George's little shelter for a moment. "Huh. Okay, guess I'll be back here just before dawn then."

"What? Why?" I sputtered.

He shrugged and stuck his hands in his pockets. "Like I said, you may be immortal, but you're probably not impervious." He tipped an imaginary hat to me too, echoing George's gesture. "Lock your door," he called over his shoulder as he walked away.

"Thanks for caring," I whispered to no one in particular.

CHAPTER SEVEN

I stood just inside the back door and listened to the building. I heard nothing, which I hoped meant that Poe was still reading upstairs. If Nick ever saw him in person, he'd have no doubt it was Edgar Allan Poe in that security footage, and I really didn't want to have that conversation with him, no matter how high his tolerance was for inexplicable things.

I stopped into the storeroom and called softly, "Poe? Are you in here?"

There was no answer from the nest, so I opened the door and peeked in. It smelled faintly of vomit, but Poe seemed to have cleaned it up himself. I dropped the twin mattress down and quickly made the bed with the bottom sheet I kept on the shelf. Then I went into the bar and heated up some soup I'd gotten for George two days before and brought it upstairs to the library with some bread.

Poe was stretched out on the sofa reading and sat up suddenly when I walked in. I placed the food on the coffee table near him and then sat. "Talk to me about spirals," I said.

He tore off a chunk of bread and had taken a bite before he suddenly paused and looked at me with a flush of embarrassment. "Forgive me for not waiting. I forgot…"

Wisely, he didn't finish the sentence that I was sure would have sounded something like, 'I forgot that you're a lady.'

"Eat," I waved him on.

He marked the page in his book and made an effort to take slow, deliberate bites of the food. "What about spirals?"

"They're a theme. Clocks have them, staircases have them. Spirals seem to be present in nearly every one of your stories or poems that features time."

He stopped eating mid-bite and considered my words. After a moment he resumed. "Hmm. I had not considered that."

"I wonder if it might be a spiral that Clocks you to different times," I said as I picked up a pencil and the notebook I'd taken notes in before and handed them to him. "Here, draw what you think a spiral looks like."

I didn't have anything more to go on than a gut instinct, but something told me that this was the right direction in which to focus our attention.

Poe turned to an empty page and began to idly sketch between mouthfuls of soup and bread. "What does it mean, to 'go running' as you said earlier?" Poe asked. "Is it some sort of euphemism for an unsavory nighttime activity?"

I stared at him. "An unsavory nighttime … are you back to accusing me of being a prostitute?"

"I merely asked a question," he answered primly.

It was with a force of will that I kept my tone of voice calm. "I run for exercise, and as I sleep during the day, nighttime is my only opportunity to do so."

He was silent as he sketched, and I could see five interconnected spirals take shape on the page. "I have given further thought to the conversation we began about the man who sleeps in the street behind this building," Poe said.

"So have I," I said. "Thank you for bringing it to my attention."

He frowned at my thanks, as though graciousness didn't fit my profile. "Have you, by chance, read *The Masque of the Red Death*?" he asked, looking up from his drawing to meet my eyes.

"Years ago," I admitted. "I know the basic story."

He arched an eyebrow at me as though he didn't believe that I'd read it. I sighed and then elaborated. "A rich prince throws a big party for all his courtiers during a time of plague. He locks everyone else out of his castle so they can't spread infection to his guests, who eat and drink and dance like they are the only people in the world. But then a masked guest comes out of nowhere, and when the prince chases him through all the rooms, it turns out the guest with the mask is actually death, and all the guests fall down dead with the plague. Beyond that, I don't remember many details except the clock, as we discussed earlier, and the circular shape of the seven party rooms in the prince's castle."

Poe had the grace to look impressed. "The first time the story was published, in 1842, I titled it *The Mask* – M-A-S-K – *of the Red Death*. Then, when I had the opportunity to republish with some corrections, I settled on the title *The Masque* – M-A-S-Q-U-E – *of the Red Death*. Can you guess why?"

"To shift the emphasis from the face covering that was hiding death to the party where the rich were hiding from death?" I guessed.

Poe raised an eyebrow in surprise, and then huffed a tiny laugh. "You continue to astound me, Mistress Ren, with your grasp of concepts which … others of my acquaintance are unequipped to see." He sipped his cold tea and considered me.

"My wife and I had moved back to New York, where the class distinction between those with means and those without stood in sharp relief. Virginia had been ill with tuberculosis for three years then, and death was an inevitability that loomed large in our lives."

I knew that his wife had died from tuberculosis in 1847, which for him was two years ago. He continued, and I realized I was being treated to a kind of literary analysis from the author himself.

"In my story, death and its many guises was not the enemy."

Poe stood and walked to the window, where he looked down at the shelter George had constructed for himself. "The true antagonist of *The Masque of the Red Death* was the masque itself – the display of wealth and greed and privilege that allows the few to lock themselves away from the plight of the many."

He turned back to face me. "Is there also, perhaps, an element of fear that contributes to your self-isolation tendencies?"

"You ask me as though I have removed myself."

"Have you not?" he asked.

I scowled at him. "I own a bar. I interact with people – all kinds of people – every night."

"You serve them drinks. You take their money. That is a transaction rather than a connection."

I didn't like his tone or his accusation. "I connect with people every time I ask about their day, or whenever I steer the conversation toward something meaningful – which I do regularly and with such subtlety that people rarely realize they've opened their minds to a new idea."

Poe looked back steadily. "Whom do you see reflected back at you from those interactions? Do you see yourself? Because in my experience, we only exist as we are in relation to others. I am a writer because I write, but my stories are only as meaningful as the meaning others have found in them. You are a bartender because you tend a bar, but do you allow others to experience the reader, the thinker you are here, behind your closed doors? Are you really those things if you do not share them with others? Or …" he must have seen the expression on my face shutter, because he sighed, "perhaps I should observe you working in your establishment before I cast judgments about your connections with other people."

"Maybe you should," I spat back, before promptly thinking better of it. "Actually, you can't. Your image was captured on a video inside a pawn shop, and the police are looking to arrest you for the break-in."

He stared at me. "You have strung together words I don't understand in a way that is meaningless to me. A video? Captured?"

I pulled out my phone, willing myself to let go of the annoyance his smug observations of my self-isolation tendencies had inspired. I navigated to the security cam footage on the police website and pressed play.

Poe stared in shock at the digital black-and-white image of himself stumbling through what appeared to be the storage cellar of the pawn shop. "What is this?" he whispered, horrified.

"It's called technology, and I shouldn't have shown you. Except that other people have seen this footage now, so it's not safe for you to be out in public while they're looking for that man," I stabbed a finger at the screen.

"No," he said, touching the screen. "What is *this*?" He pointed to the wall he had just stumbled away from on the screen. I froze the image, then screenshot it and zoomed in. It wasn't enough, so I navigated to a photo editing program, imported the screenshot, and added contrast to the photo as Poe looked between me and the screen on my phone with amazement.

There, as barely visible scratches on the brick wall, was the unmistakable image of five interconnected spirals.

"Oh," I exhaled softly as I realized I must be looking at a Clocker portal – the time travel spiral that had transported Edgar Allan Poe from 1849 to now. I met his eyes. "That's how you came through."

"Yes," he said slowly, "but how do I return?"

CHAPTER EIGHT

I sent Poe back to the nest with a quilt, a pillow, and a stack of books from my library. I locked him in with the explanation that people would be cleaning the bar during the day. The fact of the matter was that I still didn't trust him not to leave the building while I slept, and no amount of alarms or sirens would wake me after the sun came up.

Once he was tucked in, I unlocked and opened the back door. The pre-dawn darkness was my favorite time, when everything about the day was still possible, and circumstances and moods hadn't asserted themselves on the best laid plans. I stood for a moment just breathing in the damp air and enjoying the silence of the dark.

"You don't look like you slept at all." I almost leapt out of my skin when the voice came from the darkness like a disembodied ghost. Then I saw Nick leaning against the wall beside my back door, and I wanted to hit him. I settled for ignoring him. "Hey George," I called down the alley, "the door will be unlocked for about ten minutes. Bathroom's on the left down the hall. Then meet me in the bar and I'll give you breakfast."

I looked at Nick and realized he hadn't slept either, so I relented. "You want coffee, or something to put you to sleep?"

He grinned at me, and despite the tired lines etched in his face, there was a mischievous sparkle in his eyes. "I'll take whatever you're offering."

I couldn't help the smile as I turned to head back inside. Nick followed me into the bar, where I turned on an electric kettle and pulled out two mugs.

"You're not having any?" he asked.

I shook my head. "I'm heading to bed as soon as I lock up."

He sat at his usual barstool across from me and then nodded his head toward the hall. "Why are you doing it?"

I raised an eyebrow. "George?"

"Yeah."

I shrugged. "If not me, then who?" It had been too long since I'd said those words, and I savored the taste of them – slightly sweet, slightly tart, with a hint of satisfaction.

I pulled a couple of packets of oatmeal out of a drawer and poured them into a bowl, then I measured espresso grounds into a French press.

"Don't you have to work today?" I asked Nick as I added boiling water to the coffee.

He shook his head. "Day off. Want to do something?"

"I'll be sleeping, and so should you," I said without my usual disclaimer about dating customers. "What are they doing about the pawn shop guy, by the way?" I asked with the subtlety of an elephant. Nick didn't seem to notice though.

"The owner's been sleeping in the shop with a loaded gun," he scoffed, disgusted. "What could possibly go wrong?"

The pit in my stomach that had been there since Poe stumbled into my bar yawned wider, and I fussed with the French press just for something to do with my hands.

"Can I ask you something, Ren?"

I shrugged. "Sure."

"How is it you've owned this building since it was built in the 1840s?"

My heart hammered, but my hand was steady as I poured the coffee into two mugs. "The land was deeded to a trust set up for the first Alexandra Reynolds by her father, and all the firstborn girls in my family were named after her. Naming me after that long-dead grandmother ensured that the title never has to transfer out of the trust."

I turned to hand him his coffee. "Why were you looking at my property records?"

He shrugged. "Because I can. Because I'm interested. Historic architecture in this city is a hobby, and this is a cool building."

George shuffled down the hall and stopped before entering the main bar.

"Come in, George. Grab your coffee, and I've got some oatmeal and fruit too," I said as I poured the hot water into the bowl with the instant oatmeal.

I had no idea how old George was or how long he'd been homeless. He'd just showed up in my back alley one day, and after about a month it became clear he would stay for the summer. So I asked his name and started bringing him whatever bar snacks I had left over each night. George dismantled his shelter whenever the first frost hit and returned again each spring to rebuild. I'd never asked him where he wintered, and until now, he'd never come inside.

"George, this is Nick. Nick, George."

With his face scrubbed clean and his wet hair pushed back off his face, George's probable age went from indeterminate to somewhere in his forties. He nodded warily at Nick, then shuffled to the bar to pick up the mug and the bowl. "Thank you, ma'am."

"Have a seat," I said, indicating a barstool next to Nick. George eyed it, then shook his head.

"If it's all the same to you, ma'am, I'd prefer to take my food outside." He didn't meet my eyes and shuffled his feet uncomfortably.

"No problem," I said, putting two bananas and a bunch of grapes in a bag. "I'll open the back door again at sunset. You're welcome to use the bathroom whenever I don't have customers."

George seemed to consider Nick for a long moment before he finally nodded, as if to himself, and then met my eyes. I was struck by how old they looked, even in the face of a fairly young man, and the amber color made him look wild somehow.

"You're very kind, ma'am," he said simply.

I sighed. "No, I'm very tardy. I'm sorry it's taken me so long to offer."

George picked up the bag and the dishes in one hand, then tipped his imaginary hat to me with the other. "I'll watch the door while you sleep," he said, and he flashed me the smallest smile as he left, which made him look even younger still.

Nick watched George go, and when he heard the back door close, finally turned back to face me. "What do you know about him?"

I shrugged. "He showed up about five years ago, stays the summer, and winters somewhere else. That's what I know."

He shook his head. "I can't figure you out. You leave the door open for a homeless guy you know nothing about, but I come and sit at your bar every night for two years, and I don't get an invitation."

Nick's teasing always came with a smile, and suddenly, I was too tired to defend against him. So I smirked. "Nick Pieretti, I invite you to use my bathroom whenever I don't have customers."

He laughed, then impulsively stood, leaned over the bar, and gave me a kiss on the cheek. "I'll take you up on that. Sleep tight, Ren, and lock up behind me."

I resisted the urge to touch my cheek and walked him down the hall. He stopped at the men's bathroom and opened the door. "No shower," he said, closing it.

I shook my head. "I have one upstairs but I'm not really—"

"No," he said quickly. "My brother-in-law sells pre-assembled shower stalls for trailers. If you have a room with plumbing that I can steal part of, I'll put one in for you."

I stared at him. "There's a supply closet I don't need right next to the bathroom. Why would you—" I didn't know how to finish that question because I wasn't quite sure what I was asking.

"George didn't sit down because he knows how he smells, and sink washing isn't going to cut it. You were going to let him upstairs into your space, and I'd feel better if you kept your altruism downstairs, because I'm protective about my friends," he grinned tiredly, "even the ones who won't date me."

He continued walking toward the back door. "I'll bring some clothes by that should fit him, and if you're willing to throw his things into the laundry sometimes, he might be willing to eat inside."

I exhaled softly. "Thanks, Nick."

He stopped to face me before opening the door. "Sleep tight, Ren."

"What changed your mind about George?" I asked.

Nick's eyes searched mine for a long moment, and I tried not to feel his gaze in my stomach, but it had nonetheless begun filling a little of the pit that was there. "He sized me up," he finally said.

That surprised me. "What?"

"He's protective of you, and he sized me up. When he decided I wasn't a threat to you, he took his food to go."

"How—?"

"Cop eyes." Nick kissed my forehead. "Don't let the bedbugs bite."

"Dream wonderful dreams or dream nothing at all," I added automatically.

He smiled. "That's a good wish," he said before he closed the door behind him.

I waited a moment by the door listening to Nick murmur something to George. When there was silence again outside, I turned my senses in. All was quiet in the building, and for the first time in a very long time, my mind was quiet too.

CHAPTER NINE

For a Tuesday night, The Door was busy, and I was glad I'd asked Macey to come in. I had hoped to be able to take off early for a spiral-hunting expedition with Poe, but between a bowling league tournament win and a surprise birthday party, we didn't stop running until I locked the door behind her at 2:10am. And as tempted as I was to sit down in my chair and curl up with a good book, I found both chair and book occupied by my uninvited guest when I finally made it upstairs.

I had locked Poe in my library while the bar was open, and when I went to check on him, it seemed his only movement, given the size of the stack of books next to him, had been between the bookshelves and the chair. There was a notebook and pencil next to him, but his attention was deeply engrossed in the pages he was reading.

Poe looked up from his book. "I believe, when I wake up from this dream, that I shall never again presume to believe I know aught of the world."

I looked at his reading material of choice and almost laughed out loud to see *1984* in his hand.

"I had the thought," I said as I handed him the container of fried rice, "that I shouldn't take you with me tonight when I go hunting for spirals." I'd taken the other half of the food out to George, who'd been reading a two-day-old newspaper by the light above the door. He'd thanked me kindly for the meal and told me to keep an eye on my paper products in the coming months because the price of oil had gone up so much the supply chain could be affected.

Poe looked up in surprise from the rice. "How will you know whether it will work?"

"I have the drawing you made, and I can wander around nighttime Baltimore a lot less conspicuously than you can. If I find one, I'll come back and get you, but until then, you can stay here and safe from anyone who might recognize you as the security cam guy, or worse, as yourself."

"Why, pray tell, would that be worse?" His voice had the edge of an offended man, and whatever ease we'd managed to find with each other was suddenly tenuous.

I stared at him for a long moment, then tried to listen to my words as though I were him. "Time travel is not a normal or expected phenomenon, and the very few people who can do it are careful to keep their ability a secret. So, while it is true that there are people who would be utterly thrilled to meet *the* Edgar Allan Poe, there are also people who would see you as an oddity to be studied, or worse, to be feared. Those are the people who would have you locked up 'for your safety,' and certainly you would be poked and prodded and tested to see what's different about your blood and your immunities and your genetics. And that's just because you're from the past, never mind that you happen to likely be a Clocker."

He looked away, as though weighing my words. "So, I could perhaps find renown in this time because, as you say, my work has persisted and possibly grown in audience and appeal these last hundred and seventy years. But the fame would almost certainly come at the cost of my freedom, and perhaps even my liberty."

"Exactly," I said.

"Or I could return to my time and live out the remainder of my days entertained by the knowledge I've gained from my sojourn in this extraordinary time, surrounded by the familiar, albeit unremarkable, world that I know." There was a glint in his eye when he studied me. "Perhaps I will one day write a story about a woman trapped behind a wall with nothing but her books to keep her company, and the quest for a doorway to the past that set her free."

I scoffed, "Didn't you once say, 'The death of a beautiful woman is the most poetical thing in the world,' or something like that? I'm guessing I should be worried."

"Oh, I doubt that I would see to her death. It would be far more satisfying to torture her with the anticipation of seeing how she'd been immortalized." The amusement in his eyes was real, and I barked a laugh at his look of gleeful anticipation.

That Edgar Allan Poe appeared to have a sense of humor was almost as remarkable to me as the fact that he had teased me, and I was startled to realize that I was growing to like him.

"You'll stay here, out of sight of the window, while I'm gone?" I asked.

My question seemed to sober him. "I cannot claim to like that you put yourself at risk for my sake, Mistress Ren, but I will own that I appreciate it very much."

"And I," I said with complete sincerity, "appreciate that my books are getting so much love from you. I will admit that it has felt a bit selfish of me to keep them for my own use. Thank you for reading them."

He smiled a genuine smile then, and it transformed his face. "I am able to admit when I am wrong, and about you, Mistress Ren, I was mistaken in earnest. These books are more than just words on a page to you. They are knowledge, love, reason, laughter, adventure, pain, mystery, and even fear."

He looked proud of me, and of himself, for recognizing who I was inside my gender and my race. But his expression became serious as he continued. "The challenge, when one is as enamored of the lives one can lead in books as you and I are, is to find our way off the shelves so as to experience our lives first-hand." He waved a hand around the library. "One could certainly spend one's entire life within these walls and feel that one has lived. Yet, I would argue that with intimate knowledge comes intrinsic understanding. That I have loved gives meaning to the love I experience in a book.

That I have experienced fear gives shape to the fear in the story. That I have felt pain makes the pain on the page real."

"I have loved, feared, and felt pain," I said quietly, hearing the unspoken words *too much* echoing in my ears.

Poe met my eyes, and his gestures stilled. "Of that I have no doubt." Neither of us moved as he held my gaze. "I do believe, however, that like the muscles in your body which you seek to exercise, your life must continue to be experienced in order to be meaningful."

I felt Poe's words settle in and stick to the walls of the pit in my stomach. They felt substantial in the hollowness there, and the truth of them had weight.

The weight unbalanced me, and moving had always helped me find my balance, so I nodded, then grabbed my coat and keys. "Back in a few hours," I said.

He settled back into my chair, picked up the book he'd been reading, and didn't look up as I closed the door behind me.

CHAPTER TEN

The back alley felt empty, and I wondered idly where George had gone. My Mini Cooper was parked in a lot one street over, so I decided to detour past the pawn shop, just to see if any obvious circumstances had changed. I approached the building from the alley and noticed the curtains twitch on the upper floor as I passed the front door. A light was on upstairs, and I thought I saw a shadow move in the room. Mike was definitely home, and between the new locks on the doors and the likelihood of a frightened, gun-wielding man on site, I couldn't see any way for Poe to get back into that shop.

I pulled the hood of my sweatshirt up for whatever anonymity it offered and continued walking toward the lot where I kept my car.

My mind kept replaying select words from the conversations I'd had with Poe and Nick, until new phrases began to repeat in my brain. *Live your life. Love your life. Live … Love …*

"Hey! You!"

I'd been so intent on the words chanting through my brain that I forgot my hands were still in my pockets when I whirled suddenly to face whoever had yelled at me. There was a gun pointed at my face, and it was the only thing I could see in the dim light.

"Get your hands out where I can see them," the man growled.

Adrenaline surged through me, and I forced breath deep into my lungs to calm the panic that produced a strong instinct to run and take my chances. I let go of the keys I was clutching, then flexed my fingers so they were spread wide, and slowly pulled my hands out.

The gun in my face wavered when my hands cleared the fabric, but then steadied again when the guy realized his advantage as I raised them up.

"What the hell were you doing? Planning to rob my place?" The man's voice sounded familiar, and I squinted past the gun to see the face of the person who held it.

"Mike? Is that you?"

The gun wavered again, but Mike didn't drop his aim. "How the hell do you know my name?"

"Police! Drop the gun!" another man yelled, and even though I recognized the voice, my panic, which had begun to settle, surged up again, because now there were two drawn guns in close proximity.

I swallowed the fear that closed my throat, and spoke in my calmest voice. "Mike, it's Ren. I own The Door, and I see you there every week. Please put down the gun so Nick doesn't accidentally shoot you." The gun wavered again. "Please, Mike."

I raised my voice. "Nick, don't shoot. It's Mike Weir. He owns the pawn shop back there," I said gesturing behind me with my head, "and he's a customer in the bar. He thought I was someone else – it's just a mistake."

Mike finally lowered the gun, and I looked over to see Nick, about twenty feet away, in full police shooter stance. When Mike finally tucked the gun under his belt at his back, Nick relaxed his stance, and I let my hands come down.

"I'm sorry I worried you, Mike," I said quietly.

Mike barely glanced at me before shifting his whole attention to Nick. "I've seen you before. You're a cop."

"That's what I said."

I could hear the annoyance in Nick's tone, but I doubted Mike could.

"Are you guys going to beef up security around here or what? I've got punks like this one hanging outside my business every night." Mike gestured to me, and I bit back the rebuke his comment deserved. The man was still armed, after all.

"I'm sure she'll remember that next time you drink in her bar," Nick said, the warning evident in his tone.

Mike waved a dismissive hand. "Not her specifically, just …"

"Her kind?" I supplied. I turned my attention to Nick. "I appreciate your help. Thank you. If you gentlemen will excuse me?"

I moved past both of them and strode down the street. I heard the murmur of their voices but not their words as I left them behind.

I'd almost reached the parking lot when I heard running feet. I tensed at the sound, but knew it was Nick even before I'd turned around.

"Wait, Ren," he said, not even breathless.

I waited, hands on my hips, not saying a word.

"Why did you go back to the pawn shop?" he asked in low tones. "What do you know?"

I studied Nick's face in silence for a long moment. He looked concerned – like a friend would. It was odd to realize I hadn't really called anyone my friend in a long time. Not even Macey, who had worked for me for a year.

"I know that the issue isn't the drunk, it's what's in Mike's basement," I finally said, startling myself, because I had told him the truth.

If my words surprised Nick, he didn't show it. He had a master poker face for someone usually so expressive. I turned and kept walking to my car, and after a second, he followed me.

"Where are we going?" he asked.

"We?" I unlocked the car door and slid inside. Nick tapped on the window of the passenger door until I sighed and hit the button. He dropped into the seat next to me.

"This is me, friend-Nick, not me, cop-Nick."

I gave him a sideways glance. "There's a difference?"

He smiled at that. "Friend-Nick is much cuter than cop-Nick. He also listens better."

His honesty surprised me. "He also talks about himself in the third person." Nick chuckled, and I decided to share some honesty of my own. "I'm looking for spirals."

His eyebrows furrowed. "Spirals? Like springs, or a wheel, or a staircase? What kind of spirals?"

"I'm not exactly sure." I pulled out my phone and showed him the screenshot of the security cam footage that I'd enhanced. "Something like this, I think."

He glanced at the screen, then up at me in surprise. "The pawn shop security footage?"

I nodded. "Look at the wall."

He studied the grainy image. "I see the spiral. Is it drawn on the wall or carved into it?"

I shrugged. "I don't know. I've never seen it in person."

He handed the phone back to me. "What's its significance?"

I met his eyes and held his gaze for a long, silent moment. "I can't tell you that," I finally said.

He considered me. "Is it dangerous?"

"Not that I'm aware of," I answered.

"And since you're looking for something like it, it doesn't have to be that exact spiral?"

I exhaled sharply. "If I thought there was a reasonable way to use that exact spiral, I absolutely would. But I just don't see how it's possible. I can't exactly go up to Mike and say, 'Show me the basement of your shop,' never mind bring … someone in with me."

"And by 'someone' you mean the Poe look-alike?" he asked.

I shook my head and then started the engine. "I'm going for a drive around the old parts of Baltimore. Get out, or come with if you want to."

He scoffed. "Of course I'm coming with you. I can play twenty questions on the subject of spirals all night."

I sighed. "And I can evade your questions all night too. Okay, let's go."

CHAPTER ELEVEN

"Amity Street," I said, answering Nick's question about our destination.

"The Poe Homes?"

I didn't answer. The housing project they'd built for blacks in the nineteen-thirties had been named for the man who had lived next door. I briefly wondered what he would think about that.

"Tell me why we're going there in the dead of night, please, just so I can be prepared."

"I told you, I'm looking for spirals on some of the older buildings in certain parts of town. I just need to check out 203 Amity Street."

He cocked his head sideways. "The museum is closed, and there's no way you're breaking inside."

I said nothing, not wanting to lie or explain. Nick was silent for a lot of the ride, finally speaking just as I turned onto Amity Street.

"It's actually Edgar Allan Poe on that video, isn't it?"

I pulled over to the side of the road and turned off the engine. When I said nothing, Nick looked out the window at the brick façade of number 203. His expression was full of wonder as he put words to thoughts that seemed impossible. "Poe was in that pawn shop, and you think the spiral has something to do with how he got there."

It wasn't a question, and Nick seemed to take my silence as confirmation. I wondered if his easy acceptance of the inexplicable would ever extend to me, and then I put that thought out of my mind immediately.

He touched the window, still lost in thoughts of Poe. "He only lived here with his aunt and cousins for a couple of years, you know, early in his life, after he got himself expelled from West Point."

"Why do you know so much about Edgar Allan Poe?" I asked, genuinely curious.

Nick shrugged. "He's part of Baltimore's history, and I know my city. I know, for example, that this house was scheduled for demolition in the 1930s, and it took some serious sleuthing with old maps for the Poe preservationists to prove that this had been his house."

"And now it's in the middle of the projects," I said, peering through the window at the low brick buildings that surrounded the old row house which was now the Poe museum. I started the car and Nick looked sharply at me.

"What are you doing? I thought we were searching for spirals."

I shook my head. "Like you said, it's the projects, and you'll follow me in if I go, so …" I shrugged.

He looked at me for a long moment, and then I heard rather than saw his smile as I pulled away from the curb. "You'd care if something happened to me."

I scowled. "You're a human being. Of course I care." I steered the car back toward the river, taking side streets through older neighborhoods.

"So, were you born in Baltimore?" he finally asked me.

"I was," I said, careful to keep my voice neutral and my eyes peeled on the road.

"Have you always lived in Fells Point?"

"I've lived all over," I said, "but I moved back here about ten years ago. What about you?" I asked, because people liked to talk about themselves. It usually made them forget to ask questions.

"I grew up in Bolton Hill. My parents still live there," he said. "Are your parents still in Baltimore?"

I shook my head. "They died a long time ago," I said. "My grandmother raised me, and I inherited the building I live in from her."

"I'm sorry," he said quietly. "Any siblings?"

"No." I didn't elaborate.

He was quiet for a long moment before he finally said, "That must be rough – being alone."

"I'm used to it," I responded.

"I've got a huge family if you want to borrow any of us for holidays and family reunions. We're pretty good at them."

I stopped at a light, my heart suddenly constricting uncomfortably in my chest. Nick heard the silence and turned to face me. "Too much?"

I nodded. "Too much." I exhaled a sigh. "I don't know you, Nick, and you don't know me."

"I want to, though," he said quietly.

"You can't," I said, even more quietly.

He blew out a breath. "George said you'd say something like that."

My voice was sharp. "George? What did he say?"

Nick hesitated for just a moment, as though he didn't want to say the words out loud. "He said you had lots of reasons for being alone, but none of them were good enough to keep me away if I really wanted to get to know you."

"Really." My tone was hard. "Why are you here, Nick?" I didn't look at him, but could feel his gaze on me.

"You're mysterious and interesting," he said, "and I've never been able to resist an interesting mystery. The fact that you're beautiful too – that's actually just annoying, because it's so damn distracting."

I narrowed my eyes. "So you want to … solve me?"

He scoffed, "Hell no. Digging for clues is as much as I could ever hope for."

I cocked my head to the side and glanced at him. He met my gaze unselfconsciously, and his eyes seemed to dance in the streetlights.

"Got any other suggestions of places to look for a spiral?" I turned my gaze back to the street.

His smile was slow and easy and held no discernable intention or expectation. "The older, the better, right?"

"Pre-Civil War would be best," I said with a grimace.

"Pratt Street then," Nick said confidently.

A familiar shudder went through me, and Nick raised an eyebrow.

"Someone walk on your grave?"

I gave him a side-eye glance. "You have no idea."

I parked the car in the lot near my place and we headed to Pratt Street on foot, scanning the bricks of old buildings for spiral shapes on our way. Nick explained the history of Pratt Street and the locations of several known slave markets along it.

"Have you ever heard of the slave jails?" he asked when we got to the corner of Pratt and Howard.

"There was one right here," I said quietly, "called a slave pen. They finally tore the building down in the 1930s."

Nick scowled. "I've read some of the archives from before the Civil War. Some guy advertised that owners could check their slaves in to be fed and 'housed' for twenty-five cents a day."

"Slatter," I said under my breath.

"What's that?" Nick asked.

"Hope H. Slatter. He built the slave pen here. My nana …
knew someone who'd been held there as a child. She wouldn't walk
down Pratt Street. Too many ghosts, she said."

"Your grandmother Alexandra Reynolds?" Nick asked.

I shook my head. "No, Nana was my mom's mother. She died
when I was little."

I shuddered again as we passed the site of another pen that had
been owned by Joseph Donovan. There weren't many slave trade
buildings left in Baltimore, but nothing could erase the echoes of
pain that infused the landscape down by the Inner Harbor.

"I'd love to talk to you about your family history," Nick said
after we'd walked in silence for several blocks.

I shoved my hands into my pockets and resisted the urge to
flip the hood up on my sweatshirt. "My nana's people were
enslaved. My other grandmother's people owned them. I was too
young to ask Nana for her stories, and my parents wouldn't tell me
any that they knew. The only person in my family I ever really got
to know was Grandmother Alexandra, and she wasn't easy."

"Do you have any of their papers? Letters or photographs or
anything else a Baltimore history buff could rifle through?"

I turned to face Nick. He looked so eager and hopeful, and I
knew this was going to hurt. "It's my family we're talking about, not
abstract names in a history book. They were real people with real
lives, and their stories are personal and private to them. I told you
about Grandmother Alexandra's legacy to me because you asked

about the building. But if you ask about her life, I'm going to say no. Who she was in her life was her story to share, not mine."

"I've disappointed you."

"I am disappointed," I said, "but it's not specific to you. I've seen too many personal letters taken outside the context of everything its author had seen, done, and lived through, scavenged to fit some historian's version of the author's life. The contents of those letters aren't just facts on a page, they're thoughts and feelings, hopes and dreams. They're private, Nick. You wouldn't read someone's journal just because you had the luck to find it, would you?"

His eyebrows furrowed. "If they're dead, what does it matter?"

"Not everyone's … descendants are dead." I stumbled over the sentence and sucked in a breath at my own carelessness.

Nick turned and continued walking, and I fell into step next to him. "I'm sorry," he said. "I didn't mean to pry."

I exhaled away my frustration. It was tiring to relive. "You didn't know you were prying," I said quietly.

We didn't speak again until we turned down the alley to the back of my building. "I'm trying," he said, "to figure out how to get you and Poe into the basement of the pawn shop without getting shot, arrested, or losing my badge."

I stared at him in astonishment. "Why?" I asked simply, because the rest of the sentence tripped over all the questions that word encompassed.

He seemed to ponder his answer for a moment as he looked down the alley at George's shelter. "A couple of reasons," he said as he finally met my eyes. "As much as I am dying to ask the man about his life, not to mention all my questions about how and why he's here, it does seem pretty reckless to mess around with the universe by keeping Edgar Allan Poe."

I snorted, "You think?"

Nick grinned at my reaction, but then his smile dimmed as he looked in my eyes. "Also," he said, "I think you'd probably try to get Poe into the pawn shop on your own, and considering how terrified that guy Weir seemed to be, I'm pretty sure someone would get shot. Though honestly, I'm not so sure he'd survive an encounter with you." The grin was back, and I scowled at him.

"What exactly are you saying, Officer Pieretti?"

"I'm saying," he took the key out of my hand and unlocked my back door, then opened it and gave me back the key, "that I'm pretty sure you have secret superhero skills that nobody knows about."

He stood too close and was way too interesting-looking to be that close. I couldn't look away. "And you know that because …?"

Nick looked down into my eyes, and his tone shifted from playful to serious. "I saw you defuse the situation with Weir. You did it with words, and you did it with confidence. I know what kind of hatred is out there, and my gut tells me Weir is one of those 'shoot first, justify later' guys. But you not only saved your own life, you de-escalated the two white guys with guns. Now, you either actually are immortal, or you have the nerves of a stone-cold negotiator and the instincts to match."

I blinked at his insightfulness, and then wasn't sure what to do with the feeling of having been *seen*. It had been so long since I'd felt visible that I'd forgotten the flush of its warmth on my skin. Like standing close to a campfire on a cold night, it was addictive, but one step closer would make it dangerous. Nick *saw* me, and because I wanted to bask in the warmth of it, I took a step backwards, away from the flames.

"Or maybe I'm just a bartender who understands people," I said, forcing lightness into my voice.

He let me keep the distance I'd put between us. "I'm not going to ask if you want me to hang here while George uses the facilities, because I know you don't need my help. But if you'd like the company, I'm good for it."

I shook my head. "Thanks for helping me look for spirals." I stepped inside the back door. "Good night, Nick."

He hesitated just a second, like he wanted to say something, but then he just smiled. "Sleep tight. Don't let the bedbugs bite."

I smiled back. "Dream wonderful dreams or dream nothing at all."

I was still smiling as I closed and locked the door, and after George had come and gone with a doff of his imaginary cap and Poe was locked safely into the nest with his notebook and a new stack of books, I realized I still felt the warmth of being seen, and stepping back from the fire hadn't diminished it at all.

CHAPTER TWELVE

"Your guest sure does read a lot," George said to me the following evening when he came into the bar to get the soup I'd heated for him.

I froze, but then forced myself to behave normally. "My guest?"

"The guy who stays upstairs while you're working. He goes back and forth to the bookshelves all night. And I'm not the only one who's seen him."

My voice was calm and even. "You want to sit here and eat?"

George shook his head. "No ma'am. Your cop's seen him, but he's alright. You'll want to be watching out for that pawn shop man though. He seemed awful interested in your second-floor window last night while you and your cop were out. Got a photo of your guest too."

I packed the soup into a bag with a spoon, napkin, and some bread, and was grateful my hands didn't shake as I pushed the bag across the bar. "Thank you for keeping an eye on things, George."

"I told your cop about it already, and he told me he'd put someone to watch while you slept. He was on duty today, or he would've been here himself."

My brain was spinning through every possible consequence of Mike having seen Poe in the window of my building. He wasn't going to let it go, and the chances of him bringing the police in to search were too high to ignore. Even if they never found him, I would go from unnoticed, right past visible, straight to *examined* in record time.

"I'll keep watch on the back tonight, but I wouldn't be too sure trouble won't come right in the front door." George picked up the soup, tipped his imaginary hat at me, and left.

When I heard the back door close behind him, I ran down the hall and locked it, then sprinted back to the storeroom to unlock the door to the nest. I knocked, but then opened it and stepped inside.

"Poe?" I said, trying to keep the worry from my voice.

Poe lay on his bed, stretched out on his back with his feet crossed at the ankles. He was reading a letter written on old paper, and there were several other letters lying on the bed next to him. He looked at me, perhaps startled by my appearance there. "Mistress Ren." He sat up quickly. "Have you seen these wondrous missives? I discovered them quite by accident behind a brick cut with a curious mark."

He indicated a brick on the floor and the hole in the corner of the wall, down near the floor, where it had been. A hard edge sharpened my voice. "Those are not for your reading."

He looked surprised by my tone. "Whyever not? They appear to be quite old and have certainly lain here unread for many years."

"They may be unread, but they are not unknown, and I'll ask you to please give them to me." I held out my hand for the letters.

Poe considered me for a moment, then squared his shoulders. "No."

"Excuse me?" I stared at him.

"I beg your forgiveness, Mistress Ren, but the authors of these words have borne witness to experiences I could never have imagined."

"The words are private," I said angrily.

"Words written were meant to be shared – whether with one recipient or many, the intent was the same. To deny the words their access to light is to deny the author his voice."

"Hers," I said. "Most of those letters were written or dictated by women."

"Then it is, as I am learning from you, of even greater import that they be held up to the sun for their truth to shine in the darkness that has obscured them from history." He gathered the letters and tucked them back into the hole in the wall, then replaced the brick to cover them. It was marked with a series of squares, one inside the other, called a log cabin – a code that had been used to denote a safe harbor. It's what the nest had once been, and what I was afraid it needed to be again.

"I will respect your wish that I not read them now, but I entreat you in earnest, bring them into the light, Mistress Ren. Return a voice to the people whose stories are chronicled on those pages. I," he said, looking at me with a direct gaze, "will only be remembered by my words, and the words written about me. I am quite certain that were my legacy to be curated by certain of my acquaintances, a very different portrait would be painted than were my own words the brush and canvas. There are portraits to be drawn, Mistress Ren. Let the people's own words guide the paint."

I could feel the fight drain from my body at his entreaty, and at the truth that I knew lurked in his words. I closed my eyes, then nodded. "I will do as you ask. Read them if you like, but put them back in the wall, and when I've had some time to think about the best way to release them, I'll find them there."

"Good," Poe said with a smile. "You came in with a purpose. May I now inquire what it was?"

"Right," I inhaled. "I need to lock you in here tonight, for which I apologize. My friend," I was surprised to feel the rightness of the word on my tongue, "and I are working on a plan to get you to a spiral, but in the meantime, I'm afraid someone has seen you and may come looking for you in this building. No one has ever found this room by accident though, so I feel confident in your safety here."

Poe looked concerned as he stood. "I have less concern for myself than for you. If you are found to have been harboring a person of interest, will it not go badly for you?"

I stepped back out of the room and allowed myself the smallest smile. "It's nothing I haven't faced before. Go use the facilities as you need while I make you some food, and I'll meet you back here in ten minutes."

He turned one way down the hall and I turned the other, and when I'd plated some food and added a jug of water to the tray, I met him back in the storeroom.

Poe took the tray from me with a nod of thanks.

"Do you have enough to read?"

He smiled. "The muse has struck like never before, and I am giddy with the need to write."

I laughed out loud, and for a stunning moment, the strain of the past few days disappeared. "Edgar Allan Poe giddy with words is an image that will make me smile for the rest of my life."

He looked at me with something like tenderness in his eyes. "If my inspiration provokes even one-tenth the smile you've just graced me with, I shall think it the highest praise indeed."

I took a deep breath and let it out. "I'll get you home, I promise." For better or for worse, I thought but didn't say.

He entered the space between and turned to face me. "This time here with you has been an exquisite beauty, with some strangeness in the proportion, and I thank you for it all."

I pulled the door closed, locked it, and then reset the rack in front of it. I added a few cases of cognac for good measure, and then left the key hanging anonymously among the other keys by the storeroom door. "Good night, Poe," I whispered before I left the room.

The night was a quiet one, but a low-level buzz of tension followed me around the bar as I served the few customers I had. Nick came in early to make sure I knew what George had seen, but he was working and didn't stay more than a few minutes. I sent Macey home at eleven and decided to lock the door at midnight behind Paul and Marla.

"Whatever happened to that drunk from the other night?" Paul asked as I followed them to the door. Something in Paul's tone made me cautious.

"I never saw him again after I sent him on his way. Why?"

He looked uncomfortable. "I was talking to Mike Weir yesterday, and conversation came around to you and this place." Then he shrugged, as if trying to make light of it. "The drunk who stumbled in here the other night came up, and Mike thought it might be the guy who broke into his pawn shop. He thought you might have given the guy a place to stay. You didn't, did you?"

I arranged my expression to something incredulous. "Why on earth would I do something like that?"

"Yeah," Paul laughed, obviously relieved, "that's what I told Mike too. Good night, Ren," he said, then stopped and lowered his voice so he couldn't be overheard. "Watch yourself with that one, though. He's friendly just like anyone else in this bar, but he's scared. And we know what it's like when people get scared."

I nodded silently, surprised because this wasn't the kind of conversation I'd ever had with Paul. Then I locked the door behind them and tried not to let my worry that customers were talking about me override the more pressing issue that Mike could cause real problems. I wasn't worried for me – I'd taken care of myself for a very long time. But if anyone else got their hands on Poe … I needed to find a way to Clock him back, and I needed to find it immediately.

I'd already cleaned everything I could clean, so I took the register drawer with me, shut down the lights, and went upstairs to deal with money out of the view of the big bar windows.

My library/sitting room felt oddly empty without Poe, and I debated releasing him from his safe zone just for the company. But he'd been seen from the window, and the research I needed to do was best done without a nineteenth-century man reading over my shoulder.

I pulled my laptop out of the desk drawer where I'd been keeping it since Poe arrived, and began internet searches with key terms like 'spirals in Baltimore,' and 'Clockers,' and 'Immortal Descendants.' I found some photos of a graffiti spiral that matched Poe's sketch, but they were taken in an underground tunnel in Venice, California. The source blog for the photos was intriguing though. The author had taken photos of spirals throughout Europe

– a lot of them were just remnants and looked old, but some looked freshly painted, like one on one of the support pillars of the London Bridge. They were in odd places too, like a walled garden in France, and in a secret room that was discovered behind a fireplace at Bletchley Park in England.

I couldn't determine who the blog's author was because they hid their identity behind the name 'Clockwatcher,' but it was enough to confirm that the spirals I was looking for were very likely the same spirals that the Descendants of Time used to travel between times.

Then I turned my attention to the pawn shop itself. It was definitely pre-Civil War construction in the trademark red brick of the old row houses, and it stood in the middle of a block next to a big parking structure that had likely been built sometime in the last thirty years. I googled the address, but it didn't have any specific history that I could see until I searched in conjunction with the name Edgar Allan Poe.

Turned out, four days before he died, Poe was discovered nearby, apparently falling down and nearly insensible. No one knew where he'd been during the days before that, and he wasn't supposed to have been in Baltimore at all. One of the many mysteries surrounding the death of Edgar Allan Poe was that before he died, he apparently cried out the name 'Reynolds,' but no one knew why.

Of all the circumstances of Poe's death, that last fact was the most disconcerting to me.

Equally worrisome was the realization that he'd been discovered near the location of Mike's pawn shop, delirious and raving, and ill enough to require the help of a doctor. If we were somehow able to get Poe back through the spirals in the pawn shop basement, would he just end up right back in the coop with all the other drunken and drugged men with voting tickets in their pockets, waiting to be taken to vote?

My thoughts were spinning on ways to keep Poe safe as I tucked my laptop back into my desk and headed downstairs to let George in to use the toilet. I had just unlocked the door when it was slammed open. The door knocked me backward into the wall, and my breath left me in a great exhaled gasp.

Then the door slammed shut again, and the deadbolt was thrown. When I could breathe again, I looked up at the sneering face of Mike Weir and the gun he had pointed at my head.

"Where are you hiding him?" he rasped angrily.

I stared uncomprehendingly. "What are you doing?" I managed to wheeze out.

"I know you're hiding him. I saw him in here. Hell, you probably planned it together."

"I don't know what you're talking about, Mike." I pushed my voice out stronger so I didn't come across as weak or incapacitated, though I was definitely feeling off-balance. Every woman knew there was a fine line between unthreatening and victim in her response to an attack.

"Let's go." He waved the gun at me and growled menacingly. "Upstairs."

I turned and stumbled up the stairs. I could feel the dawn coming, and I was so tired. I could only be glad I hadn't unlocked Poe's door before opening the back door, and I hoped that when Mike saw that the building was empty, he would just leave and we could pretend this had never happened.

But it became clear as Mike prowled through my personal spaces that he was getting more and more agitated. "Why do you have all these books?" He spat the words as though my library offended him. "And what the hell is this? You have so many bedrooms you could turn one into a bathroom?" He stared up at the chandelier in disgust, and I was fighting the urge to curl up in a corner of my bed and hide under the covers until he left.

After rifling through my closet under the eaves and opening every door to every cabinet in the whole upstairs apartment, Mike finally whirled on me. "Where is that bastard who broke into my place? He's your partner or boyfriend or whatever – I saw him here!"

"I don't have a partner or boyfriend or whatever, Mike. I just want to go to sleep," I breathed tiredly. "Please, just leave and let me sleep."

He glared at me, a muscle in his jaw ticking with each grind of his teeth. "I'm taking you with me to the cops. They'll make you tell me where he is." He shoved me in front of him toward the steps, and I cried out in exhausted frustration. My body was beginning to shut down, and my ability to resist … anything… was going with it.

Mike did a last sweep of the bar and storeroom before unlocking the back door and pushing me out. The gun he held on me felt more dangerous than it should have because my defenses against him were so low, while everything about Mike seemed spring-loaded with fear and menace. I sincerely hoped that George was nowhere about, because I didn't trust Mike not to shoot first and ask questions later.

The sun had almost risen by the time I stumbled to my knees in the alley behind Mike's pawn shop. "Get up!" His voice was a snarl, and I closed my eyes against it.

"I can't," I sobbed, and it was true.

He growled in frustration and shoved his arms under mine to lift me up to my feet. Then he half-dragged, half-carried me to the back door of the pawn shop, unlocked it, and shoved me inside while he disarmed the alarm system. I lay where I landed, sprawled on the floor, while he struggled to reset the alarm. I didn't even have the energy for tears, and at that moment, I didn't care if he left me there on the floor, as long as I could sleep.

Mike muttered something under his breath that I didn't catch, and just as the sun came up and I felt the light peek through the dingy shop windows, everything went dark, and I was out.

CHAPTER THIRTEEN

I came to consciousness slowly, ears-first as usual. The sounds were different than I was used to – more muffled somehow. Someone was talking … upstairs? That couldn't be. I slept on the top floor of my building. Except … everything came back to me then. I wasn't in my building. The last thing I remembered was falling to the floor of the pawn shop before I blacked out.

I listened more keenly, and I heard what sounded like two men talking above me. There was movement and footsteps overhead, and then the quiet settled over the building again like a heavy blanket. I couldn't even hear the sound of clocks or the hum of anything electronic in the room around me.

I opened my eyes and saw dim light coming through a small, high window. Dim light meant either sunrise or sunset, but since I was waking up, it had to be sunset. Where was I? The basement, was it? The smell of something musty and damp assailed me and confirmed the likelihood of being underground. I sat up then and realized I was curled up on some kind of sofa amidst a jumble of furniture and junk stacked in precarious piles around the room. My eyes adjusted to the dim light, and I scanned the room for a door or a staircase out.

Panic began to crawl up my throat as I realized that if it was, in fact, evening, then Poe had been locked in the nest for almost twenty-four hours. I stood up too quickly and almost fell as my eyes searched frantically for a way out. I finally found a narrow staircase that led up, and I made my way over to it on silent feet, forcing myself to stay calm and quiet. I climbed the staircase quickly. At the top of the stairs I paused to listen again, not certain about the silence on the other side of the door. My hand was on the light switch, but I didn't dare turn it on until I determined whether I was alone.

Then I saw the shadow of feet outside the door, and my heart stopped beating and the breath caught in my lungs. The doorknob began to turn, and I stepped back against the left wall and tried to become one with the bricks. As the door opened, I considered pushing through it and past whoever was coming in. I was already up on the balls of my feet when I heard a whispered voice.

"Mistress Ren?"

All the fight drained from my body and my heart began beating again as blood whooshed through my ears. "Poe?" I whispered back.

A familiar dark head poked in through the door, and I could just see the smile on his face as he looked at me in the dim light. "You're alive."

"I don't kill easily," I responded. "And I don't think Mike intended to kill me."

"Intent is far too subject to the whims of circumstance for such confidence. I feared he may have done you harm when he realized the consequence of his actions."

Poe opened the door to the stairwell wide. "But come. You should escape this place before he returns, lest he seek to do such harm."

"Poe," I said quietly, "we're here. Somewhere in this basement is your spiral."

"Yes, I know. It is why your friend, Mr. Pieretti, brought me here when he came to escort Mr. Weir to the police station."

I could barely process his words as I turned to head back down the stairs. Nick had been here? To arrest Mike? "Come with me, and explain, please."

As we descended the steps, my hand trailed across a light switch, which, when turned on, illuminated one dim bulb in the center of the low ceiling. I hoped it wasn't enough to draw attention to the small window at the top of the wall, but I didn't want to take chances.

So, as Poe told me how George had recognized Mike then trailed us to the pawn shop, I climbed up and covered the window with the lid of a cardboard box. As we began our search for the spiral, he regaled me with Nick's discovery of the nest based on his knowledge of pre-Civil War buildings and the rumor, documented in a book about Baltimore history, that mine had been a safe-house on the Underground Railroad. The fact that Nick had not only discovered the room but found the key was cleverness I hadn't expected from him, and when Poe told me how Nick lured Mike away to the police station to identify the man who'd broken into his building, I found myself wishing he were with me as I tried to send Poe back in time.

"I find I quite liked your friend," Poe said. "He seemed remarkably well-versed in my work, and I believe I would have enjoyed speaking with him at length. It's a pity you won't allow him to court you, despite the fact that he is clearly smitten."

I scowled at him. "How do you know that?"

"Why, he said so, of course." Poe looked startled at the question. "And he was quite frantic at the idea that you could be injured. You're not, are you? Your alley-dwelling neighbor seemed certain that you hadn't been, but he seemed to believe there was a future in which you would be if we hadn't acted as we did."

"My alley-dwell— George?"

"Yes, quite. I do believe he might have a touch of the sight. He was most insistent that we time our distract-and-rescue plan for precisely sundown. He seemed to believe it would be our greatest chance for success on all fronts – removing the pawn shop owner from the premises and locating you. He couldn't know about our quest for the spiral, of course, but he certainly put an emphasis on our chance for success on *all* fronts."

Oh my. Apparently George and I were going to be having a conversation about who, exactly, he was.

I shifted a box out of the way and something clattered to the floor. A walking stick – no … I bent to pick it up – a sword stick. The cleverly-concealed sword within the walking stick was topped with a handle made of carved ebony in the shape of a bird's skull. I slid the sword partway out of its sheath, then turned to Poe.

"You need to take this with you," I said, trying not to laugh at the absurdity of the symbolism. "If we're successful and you return to the same place you left, it is likely to be the coop where you were beaten and forced to drink alcohol."

Poe looked around the cellar of the pawn shop at the brick walls and the low, thick-beamed ceiling. "If I were in a cooping gang, I would certainly consider this place a likely hole in which to hide my victims. I shall take your advice, Mistress, for I had not thought beyond finding the spiral itself."

"And …" I shifted the last box away from a wall I had recognized from the surveillance footage. "Here it is."

Poe stepped up beside me and studied the etching in the brick. The whole design was approximately the size of my arm from elbow to fingertips, with a center spiral and four others surrounding it in the rough shape of an equilateral cross.

He exhaled quietly, and I realized he was perhaps as nervous as I was. I turned to him and started to speak, "I don't know—"

"Mistress Ren," he began quietly as he met my eyes. "It is by no means an irrational fancy that in a future existence we shall look upon what we think our present existence as a dream."

I smiled at the tender expression in his eyes and marveled at my sense that I was about to lose a friend. "Present and future being relative, of course," I said.

"Of course," Poe patted his shirt pocket proudly. "I spent my time in your secret room quite productively. Perhaps there will yet be a story about a woman's quest for a doorway to the past that will set her free from the walls behind which she has imprisoned herself."

I leaned forward and gave him an impulsive kiss on the cheek. "Be sure to mention the traveler who learned to see the world through new eyes."

"Ah, but the traveler is the storyteller, and the woman is the heroine who set his heart and mind free to explore the richness of a world his narrow view had denied him."

Sadness for the future he wouldn't have hit me like a wave. "I hope I get to read it someday," I said as I stepped back so he could approach the spiral. "Be safe, Edgar Allan Poe."

"And you as well, Alexandra Reynolds."

"Do you know what to do?" I asked as he stepped forward to touch the spiral.

He began tracing the center spiral with his finger, then moved to the right one. "Yes," he said, "I believe I do." His finger followed the lines of each spiral until the end of the last one, and then he was gone.

CHAPTER FOURTEEN

Edgar Allan Poe

I woke retching, the meager contents of my stomach retained only by force of will. I was weak, and my legs trembled as I attempted to stand, and once upright, they rebelled at my first step. I was aided by the cane, which I had unaccountably retained in one hand, while my other hand patted my breast pocket. I was reassured to feel the crinkle of paper still there, and suddenly, escaping the walls which imprisoned me was foremost in my thoughts.

Mistress Ren had been correct in her assumption that I would return to the coop in which I had apparently been held. Surrounding me on the floor and against the walls were ten or twelve men in various stages of inebriation, the stench of whom filled my nostrils unpleasantly. The steps that led to the ground floor rose ominously, and the pitch black of the night outside the small window was broken only by the light of a single lantern suspended from a hook on the wall near the staircase.

I picked my way carefully through the landscape of limbs, attached, as they seemed, to their owners without discernable means of control. The men were uniformly drunk, uniformly dressed in clothing that indicated their means to be spare, and of uniformly pale countenance, as though it had been several days or even a week since they'd seen the sun.

I reflected, as I stepped past young men and old insensible with drink, that I had been among them just days before, imprisoned by men of my own race, and it was only by the grace of a woman whom I had insulted at every turn for hers that I stood now, sober and sword in hand, armed with the riches of the ages from my time spent in her library, and indeed, her company.

Emboldened with purpose, I climbed the stairs and prepared myself for battle, as whatever stood between myself and freedom could not keep me. My mind swirled with the bright butterflies of knowledge, each dancing so tantalizingly on the breeze, and each more enticing than the next. I had to wrench my mind's eye back to my purpose. Freedom of body first, then freedom of ideas and words could follow.

I paused at the top of the stairs, listening to the quiet beyond with an ear attuned to the silence of the space between the walls where I'd spent the most remarkable days of my life. No voices spoke, no footsteps fell, and no human sounds announced the occupants of the rooms beyond, so I turned the handle of the door and pushed it open, marveling that it hadn't been barred or locked, so confident were my captors in the strength of their drink.

When I stepped into the hallway, I realized the building was a storehouse of sorts, with sacks of dry goods filling the room beyond. I listened for just a moment more before I took my quest for freedom in hand and moved toward the rear of the building. I hoped that any door there might be fastened from the inside, but what I found instead was a man entering from the alley carrying jugs likely full of whatever swill kept the men below subdued.

He stared at me in horror. "You!" His shout was that of a man who couldn't believe what his eyes told him to be true, and I instinctively lunged for the still-open door. He tried to grab for me, but I knocked his hand away with the handle of my stick and pulled the door shut behind me. It would only deter him a moment, but in that moment I knew freedom.

Instinctively perhaps, or by unconscious design, I ran for the only haven I had known in Baltimore since I had shared a residence with my aunt and cousins on Amity Street. The sounds of my pursuer followed me as I turned down the back alley of Ren's building, but I was inside the door before the villain had seen me. I could still hear his shouted questions about the direction the "thief" had taken.

I hurried down the hall to the room which I knew to be full of racks and shelves. The light inside the building was different, and a flickering lantern cast eerie shadows on the casks and crates that lined the walls. The shelves that covered the door to the room between the walls held few boxes, and I was able to move them quickly. The secret door itself was not locked, so I swung it open, brought the lantern with me as I stepped inside to pull the shelves in front of the entrance, and then pushed the door closed behind me.

Breathing hard from exertion, and indeed, panic, I finally took stock of my circumstances. The space felt much the same as it had the last time I had occupied it, but it appeared rather differently. There was no mattress propped against the wall, but there were several thin bedrolls and blankets stacked in a corner. There was a flagon of water and a bedpan for waste, as well as a jar with dried bits of fruit and another with a sort of hard tack cracker. There were no books on the shelves, but there was a neat stack of paper, several quills, and a bottle of ink. In the corner of the small room, near the floor, was the brick with the square-within-a-square markings. I pulled the brick from the hole it hid and reached inside to find a much smaller stack of letters than I'd found previously. By the light of the lantern, I could see some I recognized from my last perusal.

These were the words of the enslaved who had escaped their bonds and had sheltered in this place on their way to freedom. The parallel to my own circumstances, however tenuous the thread, struck me a heavy blow that rocked me on my heels and sent my thoughts staggering.

Here, in a tiny room hidden between walls, was a place to rest, and in the brief moments of safety that were felt in this place, the people had been able to put pen to paper and create. How many stories had not been told because there was no time or strength for anything other than survival? I had experienced this, as Mistress Ren had pointed out, in times of poverty in my own life. What must that be for one who had no guarantees – whose only guaranteed freedom in life was *from* life?

I pulled the notepapers out of my pocket and picked up the quill, then considered carefully before I finally wrote the conclusion to Mistress Ren's story as it should go.

But in the end, she shaped the freedom that had been within her all along – the freedom to choose her own mind, no matter her circumstances – to fit the dreams she had for her life. And when she shared what she had chosen to think, to feel, to imagine with others, the dreams took shape and form.

And, I wrote in the voice of the traveler, *I saw in her dreams the substance of her journey, and knew then that I had not been as alone on my own journey as I had imagined.*

The sound of the shelves moving outside the door surprised me such that I dragged the quill across my signature. I hurriedly folded the story and shoved it behind the brick with the letters to keep it safe from the cooping gang should it be them outside the room, then stood against the far wall, away from the door.

It opened. I heard whispering, and then a young woman and her small child entered the space. The woman carried a piece of bread and a bit of something wrapped in paper, while the child gnawed on a late apple. The child saw me first and froze, eyes wide with terror, and the mother went very still. "What is it?" asked a voice I recognized, but should not have known.

It was not possible.

Was it?

"Mistress Ren?" I said, forgetting in my shock to whisper.

The second woman, for it surely was Mistress Ren, albeit in proper women's garb and not the scandalous trousers she'd worn during our brief acquaintance, stared at me in horror.

"Who are you?" she whispered, her fear scenting the air.

"It is I, Edgar Poe, Mistress. I mean you no harm," I said, holding my hands open before me. The young mother flinched, and I addressed her. "Nor do I mean you or your child harm. Forgive me, madam. I shall leave you to your haven."

I left the lantern behind and slipped past the shocked women out into the storeroom. Mistress Ren murmured something to the other woman and then called out to me, "Wait, sir."

I paused, my own heart pounding uncomfortably at the fear in her tone. I turned slowly, my hands still open by my sides, perhaps to show that I held nothing beyond the cane that I'd tucked under my arm. "I am sorry to have frightened you, Mistress. I should not have presumed."

"You're Edgar A. Poe, the poet," she said quietly, and I marveled at the balm her words were to my sense of myself.

"I am," I answered.

"How came you to my ... here?" Her words stumbled, as though she were new to the ownership.

How to answer, for it was clear she had no memory of me, nor should she, if in fact time was linear and days were lived sequentially. "You gave me safe harbor in that room you call a nest."

Her brow furrowed, and I thought to myself, in the way one thinks of fine art or an exquisite sentence, that she was beautiful. "When did I do that?" she asked.

I studied Alexandra Reynolds for a moment as I considered my words. She truly did not remember, and I considered the likelihood that my honesty might alter something for her. But I saw no other choice than honesty, because it was all I had left to give her, even as I owed her so much more than I could ever repay. "More than a century from now," I said quietly.

Her eyes widened in surprise. "But how could you know what I—" She broke the sentence in half and swallowed what had not yet been uttered. Then she shook her head, as if in disagreement with herself about what could be true.

Suddenly, a commotion filled the hall outside the storeroom. Fear lit behind her eyes, but purpose moved her to action as she slid the shelves into place and stood with her back to the wall as if on guard.

"There is something here, I know it," a man's voice snarled close by.

I expected the man from the coop. I braced myself to attempt to run past him again to lead him away from this haven, but when the intruder rounded the corner and filled the doorway with his bulk, I saw it was not him.

"Where are they?" He lunged, clearly intent on doing harm to the woman behind me. Without conscious thought I stepped forward and smashed the head of my cane into the man's nose, which broke most convincingly and splattered his face with blood. He howled and lunged again, this time at me, but I launched myself from the room as my original plan had dictated, and prayed he would follow me from the building.

I ran for the front door through what appeared to be a warehouse full of fabric and was gratified to hear the man lumber behind me. I called to Mistress Ren and hoped she could hear the plea in my voice. "Save yourself, for one day you will save me." I hoped only to steer him clear of the building so that she could lock the doors behind him, but just as I looked back to see her at the door, the man from the coop stepped out of the shadows and swung a club at my head.

Ren's scream was the last thing I heard before the world went black.

CHAPTER FIFTEEN

Ren

I fell to my knees as the vision of the attack on Poe swam in front of my eyes and the memory of my own screams filled my head.

"Ma'am? Are you hurt?"

George's voice carried through the echoes in my mind, and I looked up to see him hovering above me with a worried look on his face.

I glanced around. It was full night, and I was in the alley behind my building. I peeled the layers back between memory and reality and realized the truth of what had just sent me to my knees.

Poe had changed the past.

Or maybe I had.

I let George help me stand, and he opened the back door to my bar. "Nick left it open for you and told me to guard the door. He said you wouldn't have a key."

Nick and I were going to have a conversation or two about his presumption. It would involve a thank you, but there would also be an establishment of limits.

"Come in, please, George," I said as I turned on lights and steadied my legs under me.

"Yes, ma'am," he said quietly as he closed the door behind himself.

I stopped in the storeroom and turned the light on to see the shelves standing open and the door to the nest ajar. I heard George pause behind me.

"Did you see this room … before?" I asked him, wondering if he would reveal that he was a Seer.

He hesitated a long time before he finally answered. "I knew it was here."

"And that's all I'm going to get about that," I murmured under my breath. I spoke in my normal voice. "There's a refrigerator behind the bar. Please go fix yourself something to eat and then we'll talk, okay?"

"Yes, ma'am," he said quietly.

I stepped into the nest and marveled that it looked so tidy. The sheet and quilt were folded and the mattress rested against the wall. The books from my library upstairs were in a stack on the table, and the notebook and pencils were placed neatly on top.

I opened the notebook to discover that several pages were torn out, leaving only my original notes from our search for the spiral. Disappointment squeezed my chest, and I inhaled sharply. It was as though Poe had never been there. I missed him with a suddenness that took my breath away.

My eyes found the log-cabin-marked brick near the floor, and I crouched to remove it from the wall. I reached inside and pulled the stack of letters out, hoping that perhaps he'd left me a note, but the missives on top were on the familiar paper – the blanks from the beginnings and ends of my grandmother's books, carefully cut away with a sharp knife. I allowed the letters to fan through my fingers and considered the promise I'd made to Poe. Perhaps it was finally time to allow these stories to be told. I wouldn't do it myself, of course; the glare of the spotlight would be too bright on my face. But Officer Pieretti, with his passion for the people and history of Baltimore, could 'find' them and shepherd their publication.

A folded stack of notepaper, different from the rest, caught my attention, and I pulled it from the bunch. The handwriting was unfamiliar to me. It was a narrative that began with the words:

It was a night like any other, and a night like no other of my experience when I stumbled through Death's Door, insensible with drink and the beatings of men who would see me imprisoned. It was there, in a room colored with the burning orange of the setting sun, that I beheld the face which became the visage of my dreams. She wore the scowl of a woman impatient with men, and her voice calmed me even as she turned the key in the door that would become my cell.

I swallowed the sob that lodged in my throat. Poe had left me the story he'd written. The notepaper was faded with age, and although I'd never seen it before, I knew he'd hidden it there the night I met him again, so many, many years before.

Nick arrived at midnight with the pre-fab shower stall in tow, which he and George installed in the closet next to the public bathrooms while I closed and cleaned the bar. They were just finishing the caulking when I brought them hot coffee and sandwiches.

"George," I said as Nick cleaned his tools, "the space in the walls of the storeroom has a bed, electricity, and some books in it."

Nick glanced up at me in surprise, but I ignored him and continued speaking to George, who held himself very still.

"A long time ago it was a shelter for people who needed a haven, but until a few days ago, it hadn't been that in many years. It's not big, but it's safe, and it's yours if you want it."

I exhaled, surprised at how easy the words had been to say.

George seemed to move in slow motion as he finished his coffee and rinsed the cup in the sink before handing it back to me.

"I'm very grateful for the kind offer, ma'am, but I'm not sure I remember what sleeping indoors feels like. Maybe I could get back to you on that?"

I nodded. "The offer stands."

He tipped his imaginary hat at me and said, "Thank you, ma'am," before taking his sandwich and departing.

Nick wiped his hands clean on a cloth and stood up with a stretch. "That was kind," he said.

"It was overdue." I gathered the mugs and George's empty plate, and Nick followed me to the bar with his sandwich in hand.

He settled himself on a barstool across from me as I washed the dishes and set them on the rack to dry.

"I have the surveillance footage from Weir's pawn shop. It clearly shows him dumping you inside the hall and then carrying your unconscious body downstairs to the cellar. He knows I have him for kidnapping if he comes near you again."

I inhaled sharply. The surveillance footage. "Thank you."

The realization that all of my carefully constructed walls could be smashed with the public release of that tape made a flush of heat crawl up my spine. But then I looked at the man sitting across the bar from me, an expression of genuine concern on his face, and I felt the closing words of the story Edgar Allan Poe had called *Death's Door* settle into the space his absence had left.

And, I saw in her dreams the substance of her journey, and knew then that I had not been as alone on my own journey as I had imagined.

"I'm not going to date you, Nick," I said, surprising myself.

He shot me a teasing smile. "So you've said."

I scowled, but there was humor behind it, and the playfulness felt light and free. "But," I said, raising an eyebrow, "I'd consider friendship." He grinned and was about to say something, but I cut him off. "I warn you now though, I'm probably moving soon, so don't get too attached."

Nick's smile faded and his tone turned serious. "Every ten years, more or less, for as far back as the records go. Wait—" He reached out a hand to stop me as I pulled back from him. "If you don't want to tell me, I won't pry. It's your story. Just know that if you want to stay this time, I can help you figure out a way." He gazed into my eyes, searching them for a clue to my thoughts. My instinct for flight was screaming at me, but with Poe's words echoing in my head, I forced myself to breathe through my panic. When my heart rate had calmed to something less bird-like, I met his eyes.

"Maybe someday I'll tell you the story of what happened the second time I met Edgar Allan Poe."

EPILOGUE

Alexandra

The newspaper said that Edgar Poe died four days later. They called his condition "mysterious," as he appeared to have been the worse for drink. No one had seen him in days, and the only word he uttered before he slipped into unconsciousness was my name, "Reynolds."

No one knew it was my name of course, as no one knew that Mr. Poe and I had spoken just before he hurled himself out into the street. The man with the club had fled, and even Mr. Timmons had left the scene rather than be associated in any way with Mr. Poe's injury. Passersby carried Mr. Poe into Gunnar's Hall, and I heard from Bess, who mopped floors there, that a doctor friend of his was called and they took him away.

I had moved Mathilda and her daughter that very night rather than risk the return of Mr. Timmons, but he hadn't come back, and since then, three more women had come and gone on their journey to leave Baltimore and the institution of slavery behind.

Slavery itself would stay with them, I knew, as it had done my mother. She carried it in her posture, in her refusal to meet the eyes of any man who wasn't my father, and in the quiet timbre of her voice. She froze at every knock on our door and taught me silence in the face of pain so as not to draw attention to us. She also taught me to stand taller than she ever could, and to speak up when she would have been silent. I had not been enslaved, but I was a freed slave's daughter, and I felt the responsibility of it to my soul.

I had other memories of my mother from my childhood – family murmurings in the dark between Mama and Nana, when the child I'd been was meant to be sleeping. Whispers about Descendants and sentences with words like 'power,' 'family,' and 'war' were layered in my memories from the time before I was taken into Grandmother Alexandra's big house.

Mr. Poe couldn't know, of course, how impactful his words to me had been. He had not realized that in all my years with Grandmother Alexandra's books, I'd searched the stories, the myths, the legends, looking for anything that revealed the secrets of the Descendants.

There were stories hinted at in the books, but the more I looked, the less certain I became that they were anything other than whispers in the dark – until the preacher came.

He began with a nighttime prayer group at the Bethel African Methodist Episcopal church up near City Hall, and then, a couple of years before I met Mr. Poe, he brought instrumental music into the Sunday evening service. Not much was known about him until his name began to be whispered by Railroad conductors and at Depots along the line. They called him the Shepherd, and the people he sent north were his flock. The silent birds in my nest began to whisper that he was a Descendant, and that he had power to grant if one were brave enough to seek it.

Immortality, they said.

I did not believe them.

But Mr. Poe claimed he'd known me a century in the future, and then he died before I could ask him how. But the whispers of time travelers and seers, shape-shifters and those who could not die had drifted through Descendant stories like smoke, and here in Baltimore was a man who might be one of them.

It was chilly, that night in October, 1849, when I attended service at Bethel and sang my love of Jesus and prayed for the freedom of my brothers and sisters. The Shepherd was tall and far too handsome, and his skin was light brown or dark white, or maybe red or tan. I thought he could pass as any race he chose, and wondered that he was choosing to live as a man who was only three-fifths of himself in the eyes of the government and barely a man at all in the eyes of the law.

I waited in the shadows outside and saw him draw the collar up on his coat against the cold. When I fell into step next to him, he didn't look surprised to see me.

"I am sorry I kept you waiting," he said in a rich baritone with a faint accent that sang with rolling hills, grapevines, and summer heat.

"They say you are a Descendant," I said, without pausing to think how strange that sounded.

He smiled. "They say you keep the birds of our flock safe in your nest." He nodded and the smile remained in his voice. "I am a descendant of my mother and her mother before her."

"Was her name Death? Because that is who they say you are from."

He might have hitched his step just a little.

"Her name was Elena, and she died long ago."

I swallowed against unexpected tears. My mother's name had been Lena, but she called me Alexandra so my grandmother would know me.

"My mother whispered about our Descendant blood, but she is dead now too. If you would teach me, I would learn to use our power to help our people to freedom."

The Shepherd was quiet a long time, and our stride began to match as we walked toward the river. He sounded thoughtful. "To which Family do you belong?"

"Family?" I asked. "I told you, my mother is dead."

He looked sideways at me. "Time, Fate, Nature, War, and Death. Which of their Families was hers?"

Something that had been buried between the layers of whispered memories sharpened into focus. "My mother once told me I was a child of War. I thought it was because my father was white."

"War," he mused, his voice drifting away in the wind from the river. "Well, that could be useful indeed." I heard the smile return to his voice.

We continued on in silence, and he seemed to be weighing something in his thoughts.

"What is your name, little bird?" he finally asked as we crossed the street to the building my grandmother had been left by her father.

"Alexandra Reynolds." I stopped and turned to him, offering my hand to shake.

"Hmm. A small brown wren with the courage of an eagle," he said, peering at me. "My name is Sebastian Tousi. I shall call you Wren," he said, "and you must call me Bas."

I heard the name 'Ren' in my mind. It was the name Mr. Poe had called me. I decided that I would be Ren now as I stepped forward into my life.

"Tell me, Bas," I said as I studied his face, "about the power of Death."

He was silent a long time, and when he finally spoke, I had the sense there was sadness in his words. "Death," he said, "is immortal."

"Is that what you are?" I asked, searching his face for something to fear, but finding nothing.

"I am love." His smile was very faint, and there was sadness in it. "And I cannot die."

I turned his words around in my mind, looking at them from every angle.

"What is my power, then? If I come from War, what can I do?"

His silence was thoughtful, and his words carried the weight of a cloak around my shoulders. "Decide what you fight for, and then choose a side. Your power will come with your choice."

I scowled. "Choice doesn't seem like much of a power."

"No?" he asked as his eyebrows rose in challenge. "Tell that to the person with none."

My skin flushed with embarrassment, but Bas put a finger under my chin and lifted it, so I met his eyes. "When you choose to fight, there will be few who can stand against you." He burned the words into my mind with his gaze, and I believed him. When he spoke again, he searched my eyes for understanding. "I know little else of your Family's gifts, lovely Wren, but when you truly come to understand the cost of immortality, it is a gift I can share with you if you choose it."

The words wound their way into my heart where they twined with Mr. Poe's plea to save myself, for I would save him, and there they sat, growing wings until they took flight and set me free.

THE REAL HISTORY

My husband told me, as I was finishing the fifth and final book of the Immortal Descendants series, that Edgar Allan Poe had disappeared for five days in 1849. He was found again in Baltimore on October 3rd, delirious and possibly drunk, wearing strange clothes and carrying a cane. He was taken to Gunnar's Hall where a doctor friend took him to a Baltimore hospital. Poe died four days later, never having regained proper consciousness except to call out for a mysterious person by the name of "Reynolds."

Of course Poe was a Clocker, and I knew I would write that story someday.

What I didn't know until I began researching Poe in earnest was how very prevalent the images of clocks and spirals are in his work. I also found a blog post that pointed out several things he wrote about that he shouldn't have known – like Richard Parker, the 17-year-old cabin boy eaten by his crewmates in *The Narrative of Arthur Gordon Pym*. Forty years after that story was written, a boy named Richard Parker really was eaten by shipwrecked crewmates. There is also Poe's prediction of the origins of the universe in the poem *Eureka* eighty years before scientists would begin to formulate the Big Bang Theory.

Poe was raised on a Virginia plantation by his wealthy, slave-owning foster parents and has been noted as an anti-abolitionist by scholars who have studied his reviews of books on the subject of slavery. He was disinherited by his foster father and often lived in poverty, just barely able to support himself, his wife, and her mother on what he earned as a writer and editor. The racist imagery and sentiment that can be found in several of his works has been studied at length, and the reversal of his views as depicted in *Death's Door* are not supported by anything other than my hopeful imagination.

The practice of 'cooping' was notorious and widespread in the late 1840s, and it is put forth as one possibility to explain the five days Poe went missing shortly before his death. Cooping gangs kidnapped poor white men off the streets, beat them, and forced them to drink to insensibility so they could keep them prisoner in 'coops,' or cellars, near polling places. They stuffed the men's pockets full of voting tickets for a certain candidate, and then on voting day, they would roll the men out to the polls, make them vote, then change their clothes and do it again until the men were finally recognized and prevented from further voting.

A scene that was written but didn't make it into this final version of *Death's Door* was set in the Old Baltimore Shot Tower, which I'd never heard of until my husband (who in the time of COVID-19 has also been my research assistant) described the process of making shot for firearms. A person climbed the spiral staircase to the top of the 220-foot-tall tower where they poured molten metal through a sieve. The 'drops' fell into a bucket of cold water on the bottom and formed perfectly round balls of ammunition. There were four shot towers in Baltimore, and at one time, this one, which still remains today, was the tallest building in the United States. I'm already planning how to add that scene to Ren's next Baltimore Mysteries adventure.

All of the facts about Pratt Street, including the locations of slave pens and the names of the men who owned them, are based on old maps and newspapers and are horribly true.

The small detail of front and end pages of books having been cut out for use as notepaper came as the result of research into 1850s letters – forgeries of which have often been made using the blank pages from old books.

Edgar Allan Poe actually did live on Amity Street for a time in his twenties, and he is buried in Baltimore. His first biography was written by a man who considered him a rival. It was not kind. I have written a small chapter in an alternate version, and whether he actually Clocked to the future during his five missing days, I leave to your imagination.

Death's Door is set in the world of the Immortal Descendants series, which begins with the Library Journal Award-winning

Marking Time. There are a few Easter eggs in *Death's Door* about some of the Clocker spiral locations, and there is one character in this story who not only appears in the Immortal Descendants series, but will also be found in his own series called A Soul's Journey, which hasn't been written yet, but fills my dreams with vivid images of tenth-century assassins.

To find out more about the Immortal Descendants series as well as my other books, please visit my website: http://www.aprilwhitebooks.com.

The Immortal Descendants Series
Marking Time
Tempting Fate
Changing Nature
Waging War
Cheating Death

The Immortal Descendants: Baltimore Mysteries
Death's Door

The Baker Street Mysteries
An Urchin of Means

The Cipher Security Series
Code of Conduct
Code of Honor

A NOTE FROM THE AUTHOR

I didn't mean to write this story at this time. I actually have two other books that were in line to be written before this one (yes, I know … Ringo!). But then COVID-19 turned the world upside down and now "normal" looks different in many big ways and a million tiny ways that none of us could have predicted about the world or about ourselves.

The book I was supposed to finish first is a romantic comedy, and my humor is more gallows than guffaws at the moment, so there were crickets where those voices used to be. Then I made the decision to put the entire Immortal Descendants series into kindle unlimited, and that seemed to want a little celebration to go with the occasion. In plotting that celebration, I imagined who Poe would encounter in present-day Baltimore. Ren's voice began tell me her story, and a whole new avenue for exploring all the little ways this time is impacting me, personally, became possible.

That being said, there is not a chance in the world that I could or would have written Ren's story without my brilliant editor and dear friend, Angela Houle. I gush about her a lot, and I'm not going to hold back this time either. I am one of those people who can absolutely take criticism, but please, please tell me what works too so I don't crawl away and hide my head under the covers. Angela delivers the perfect sh*& sandwich, with the crusts cut off and pretty garnishes, and I trust her with everything I write.

The other people without whom this story could not have been written are my husband, Ed, for his brilliant research, cover design, and constant, unrelenting support, and my friends: Rose, for her unflinching honesty, Korrie, for her excellent advice, and Rebecca, for her clear gaze and direct questions. Special thanks goes to Nicole, for her generosity, Amber, for her bravery, Dan, for his honesty, Janella, for her wisdom, and my kids, for their self-sufficiency. Special thanks also goes to Casaundra Freeman for giving Ren her voice. The audio version of this book is amazing.

And to the women and men of Kick-Ass Heroines (my reader group on Facebook ~ come join us) – your support and laughter, the dad jokes and book recs, the empowering posts about people doing wonderful things – you are just THE BEST. Thank you!

And finally, thank YOU for reading this strange story written in a strange time. I hope your new normal includes hugs from someone you care about, and conversations about things that inspire you. Turn the page for the first chapter of *Marking Time*, book one of The Immortal Descendants series, and after that, chapter one of *An Urchin of Means*, book one of the Baker Street series – both of which are set in this world, in which Time, Fate, Nature, War, and Death are Immortals, and their Descendants have powers.

And until the next time we connect, please be well, and stay safe.

Love, April

In *Marking Time* ...

Seventeen-year-old tagger Saira Elian can handle anything ... a mother who mysteriously disappears, a stranger who stalks her around London, and even the noble English grandmother who kicked Saira and her mother out of the family. But when an old graffiti tag in a Tube station transports Saira to the nineteenth century and she comes face-to-face with Jack the Ripper, she realizes she needs help after all.

Saira meets Archer, a charming student who helps her blend in as much as a tall, modern American teen can in Victorian England. He reveals the existence of the Immortals: Time, Nature, Fate, War, and Death, and explains to Saira that it is possible to move between centuries – if you are a Descendant of Time.

Saira finds unexpected friendships at a boarding school for Immortal Descendants and a complicated love with a young man from the past. But time is running out for her mother, and to save her, Saira must embrace her new identity as she hides from Archer a devastating secret about his future that may cost him his life.

CHAPTER ONE ~ CLOCKER

My mother had vanished again.

She did it every two years like clockwork, and her absence meant we'd be moving again … soon. So I did what I always did when I found the stocked fridge and the note – I ran. The knots in my guts and a startled cat were my only company as I sprinted along the top of a wall and down a dark alley. The wall ended at a narrow gap separating a head shop and tattoo parlor, and I spider-crawled between the buildings with knuckles bitten by the rough edges of the bricks. It was a free-run fueled by an early diet of superhero fiction and a fierce need to lose myself in survival mode. I dropped the last six feet, slipped into the tattoo parlor through the broken back door, and then vaulted the stair rail to hit the basement floor. My lungs burned, but my hands were steady when I stopped to loosen my backpack. I took a deep breath, slipped behind a shelving unit, and stepped into the underworld of Venice.

The prohibition era rumrunner tunnel forked into a bigger branch already colored with graffiti that felt more like one-upmanship than art. The smaller fork was jammed with boxes and pallets and other junk that kept the easy access taggers out. Old places had history, and I loved history – especially anything hidden, secret, or underground – which meant the jammed tunnel wasn't a deterrent to me; it was like an engraved invitation.

I heard the hiss of spray paint just as I turned the corner. Two bangers in respirators were throwing up tags, and though their drawing skills were decent, the tags were all gang signs and territory markers. Bangers were sheep with fangs as far as I was concerned. Anyone who needed to belong to something that badly didn't have the confidence to stand alone. And alone was all people could ever count on in life. I turned the corner and slipped through an opening at the far end before the bangers saw me.

The long, narrow passage was like my own private art gallery, with vintage tags that felt more visionary than vandalism. The standout was an old tag from 1972 signed by someone named Doran – a spiral symbol that looked ancient and vaguely Celtic. A spiral I wanted to copy.

I flipped on my Maglite and a rat darted away down the tunnel. I shuddered, imagining disease-filled fleas leaping off the creature as it ran, then focused my light on the mostly brick walls of the narrow space. There was a clean plaster facing next to Doran's spiral.

I set the Maglite on the floor, pointing up like a candle, opened my backpack, and pulled out a World War I gas mask. Besides not wanting to give myself cancer, I wore the mask to hide my face. My black hooded sweatshirt covered long dark-gold hair tied back in a braid and whatever minor curves I'd managed to grow in seventeen years. The gas mask kept me looking like any other tagger – skinny, fast, and vaguely male. Someone would have to be pretty close to see I was a girl, and frankly, no one ever got that close.

I fitted a new tip to my red can and started on the center spiral. The paint laid down easy, and by the time I got to the fourth one the tightness in my chest was letting go. The sun-like circles were a good way to mark my time living so close to the beach in L.A., and they practically painted themselves. But then things got weird: the spirals started to … glow. Like daylight peeking through the cracks in a door. Not possible with standard Krylon paint. At night. In a dark tunnel. Not possible at all. I flipped off my Maglite to see better. Maybe the fumes really were getting to me.

Something moved. The rat? I froze in place and saw a shadow at the far end of the tunnel shift. I had great night vision and I loved the dark, but shadows creeped me out. Darkness was just dark. Shadows could be anything.

Something was there and it was time to go, so my brain instantly clicked into 'flight' mode. I could drop the backpack if I had to run, but it could be a weapon too. I slid the can back inside just as a scuffling noise came from the tunnel entrance. I was trapped. By the bangers, or someone else?

"Dude, there's nothing down here." A surfer voice. Right, someone else.

"I'm telling you, man, he said it would go down tonight. We're supposed to keep the kid from running." The second whisper sounded nervous. These jokers were up to nothing good, and I backed myself against the wall to become one with the bricks.

"There's no one here. Your intel is faulty." Something in Surfer's voice changed. Like someone else just came in. Someone Surfer was afraid of.

"My 'intel' is never faulty. It's this tunnel. Tonight. Tom saw it." A third voice spoke quietly in a British accent. The Englishman's voice was slick and reptilian, and my guts twisted unaccountably.

"Dude, Tom's so scared of you he'll say you're the King of England if he thinks it's what you wanna hear. And now I'm thinkin', fifty bucks ain't gonna cut it."

"Leave now and you'll never stop looking over your shoulder." Slick's quiet menace made me shiver. I believed him, and instinct screamed at me to run.

"I wanna see what's comin'. Hit the light." Nervous Guy's voice shook.

"No light!" Slick yelled too late. The beam hit me square in the chest.

"What the hell is that?!" I was really glad I still had my respirator on. But Slick's next words sent an earthquake down my spine.

"Grab her."

I spun on the balls of my feet and sprang away down the tunnel. When I was out of range of the flashlight I reached out to both walls and did my best Spiderman impression, practically flying up the sides with all four limbs. My spine pressed against the curved brick ceiling of the tunnel, and I closed my eyes with that 'if I can't see them, they can't see me' rationale.

"Where'd she go?" Nervous Guy screeched. "She was just here!"

Slick's voice was cold in the darkness. "Get the light. She's still in this tunnel."

"No way, Dude. I'm telling you, she disappeared." Surfer walked right under me. And like most people, he didn't think to look up. It's why ceilings made such great hiding places.

I froze as Slick's flashlight beam hit Doran's spiral. He touched it gently, and then retrieved my respirator. I couldn't see his face, but I thought I'd never forget the sound of his voice.

"You can't hide from me little Clocker."

I shuddered at the threat in his words. Clocker? He had the wrong girl, and only sheer force of will kept me silent.

Finally, a few curses and a dying battery later, Slick and his henchmen slithered away.

My night vision cleared and I was alone. I spider-walked myself back down the walls and fumbled for my flashlight. I wanted to be long gone. I found my way back to the tattoo parlor through the door in the basement and was just about to sling my backpack over my shoulders when it was ripped out of my hands. I bolted for the stairs and slammed into someone beefy. "Oof!" The guy went down hard on one knee.

"Grab him!" A deep voice shouted.

Not if I could help it.

"Stop! Police!"

I closed my eyes with a sigh. This was not going to end well.

I may have lived on the edge of legal sometimes, but I wasn't a *bad* person. Yet here I was being driven home by two pissed-off cops. Officer Beef, named in honor of the massive chest that was losing its war with gravity, had hurt his knee when I accidentally ran into him and was particularly annoyed to discover I was female. Apparently, I hit hard.

"So you think you're pretty tough? Down there defacing private property." The Beef's partner was a short, arrogant Napoleon type.

"The tunnels are non-jurisdictional." The look I got from Napoleon through the back seat grate would have been less painful with a dagger attached. The Beef swallowed a chuckle and then looked out the windshield skeptically. "Windward and Pacific you said?"

"We're in the loft above the Venice Beach market."

"We?" Napoleon had a sneer in his voice I didn't like.

"My mother and me."

"Her name?" He had his notebook poised to write.

"Claire Elian."

"Father?"

"Deceased." My tone stayed perfectly even.

"Hmm. Mother's occupation?"

"Artist."

"Figures. Names her kid Saira – 'Sigh-ra' – instead of something normal and pronounceable." I didn't bother to point out he had just pronounced it.

I directed them to the back alley and led them upstairs. I already had my key in my fist, and was startled to find I didn't need it. The door was wide open.

The Beef looked sideways at me. "You leave it like this?"

I shook my head and the Beef was in front of me in a flash, weapon out, signaling to Napoleon. The main room was in chaos, with art supplies, books and papers everywhere. I followed The Beef into my mother's bedroom and sucked in a breath. Total disaster. I grabbed the key hidden at the bottom of Mom's headboard and unlocked the paint cabinet. Passports and cash were still there, but the antique clock necklace my dad gave her a million years ago was not. Napoleon entered from the kitchen. "Clear. No sign of the mother."

"She's working." The lie sat heavily on my tongue. And worse, they knew it.

Napoleon smiled. "There's the phone. Call her." Jerk.

I didn't move. Napoleon nodded at The Beef. "Once she's in I don't see much chance of her getting out, especially when they see this."

"Who? When who sees this?" I didn't like the pity in The Beef's eyes.

"Child protective services." Napoleon was dangerously smug. "They're the first call for minors."

"I'm seventeen."

"Still a minor in California."

"I have a British passport."

Napoleon snatched it from my hand. "Immigration is next on my list."

I glared at him, and The Beef must have felt bad because his tone softened. "Are you sure there isn't someone we could contact?"

I looked from The Beef to Napoleon, and bit my tongue, hard. "My mom will be back in a couple of days."

"Then she can bail you out, if she can get through the paperwork before you're assigned."

The Beef looked me right in the eyes. "We need a family member, Saira. There must be someone who can prove a relationship."

I tasted blood. There was someone.

That someone was waiting for me when I stepped off the British Airways flight in London: Millicent Elian. I hadn't seen my grandmother since I was three years old, and yet she still matched my vague memory of a tall, steely woman with iron eyes and a grim mouth. My mother couldn't stand her. Not a big surprise given the way she was sizing me up, probably wondering if I was worth the effort. Granted, I wasn't really dressed to impress in skinny jeans, combat boots, and a hooded sweatshirt. Perfect for the street. Not so impressive to a proper English noblewoman.

"I see you got his height." Millicent's tone was not flattering.

"Hello, Millicent." I knew I should be more polite and call her "Grandmother," considering she just kept me out of foster care, but she hadn't really earned the title.

"And his manners, too, evidently."

"I wouldn't know."

Millicent gave me a once-over like I was about to get wiped off her shoe. "At least you favor Claire."

"I don't suppose you've heard from my mother."

Millicent's eyes narrowed. "How long has she been gone?"

"Since Tuesday."

"Four days. She'll call tomorrow, or Monday at the latest."

I glared. "How do you know that?"

She ignored me. "I have a car waiting." Of course she did. Millicent's fancy gray Rolls Royce waited at the curb outside the airport, and her fancy gray driver held the door open for us.

"Home, Jeeves," she said with total authority.

"Jeeves? You're joking."

"I don't joke." Millicent's expression didn't change.

Jeeves caught my eye in the rear-view mirror and very slowly, he winked. It wasn't much, that wink, but it was something.

"I trust you still go to school?" Millicent's gaze was direct.

"Yes." A new one every two years. Not so conducive to making friends, which was fine with me, but it made my mother nuts. She didn't get that friends were a liability to the perpetual new kid. It was easier for me to just blend into the background, and practically a rule of thumb for a seventeen-year-old free-running graffiti artist.

"Then you shall start at St. Brigid's boarding school on Monday."

"Boarding school? I don't think so."

Millicent spoke sharply. "Our family has gone to St. Brigid's since 1554, and it's appalling to me that you've never been educated there."

"Considering you kicked my mother out of the family, it shouldn't be a surprise." I was already on thin ice – might as well see what it took to crack.

To my complete surprise, Millicent practically snorted. "I didn't kick her out of the family. She left us."

"Right." I said it under my breath, but it was full of snark and her eyes narrowed.

"Saira Emily Elian. Like it or not, you are a lady, and you will behave like a lady in my presence. Is that clear?" I looked away. My mom was not strict with me, and I was used to doing pretty much what I wanted. This thing with Millicent wasn't about my manners, it was about control. Over me. She wanted it, and I didn't want to give it up.

I fogged the window next to me with my breath and absently began tracing Doran's spiral design from the Venice tunnel, but when I felt Millicent's gaze burning a hole in the back of my neck, I wiped the window clean.

The Rolls Royce turned down a long driveway guarded by huge trees on all sides. They made me feel like a little girl stepping into a fairy tale – the kind with evil queens and enchanted forests that swallowed wandering kids into their depths. When the trees opened up, a massive building loomed in front of us. The place felt like a fortress with forbidding stone walls, and I could feel Millicent's eyes on me.

"Welcome to Elian Manor."

Marking Time is currently FREE on all ebook platforms.

Continue reading for Chapter one of *An Urchin of Means…*

The books of the Baker Street Series stand alone. They are the adventures and mysteries of Ringo Devereux in Victorian London as he keeps company with the likes of Arthur Conan Doyle and Oscar Wilde. The story of Ringo's origins as a time-traveling Victorian urchin and thief can be found in The Immortal Descendants series. Book one of that series, *Marking Time* is free and all five books are available at all e-book retailers.

CHAPTER ONE – THIEF

The little guttersnipe was fast, I'd give it that.

Quick-fingered and fleet-footed, for all it was ten years old, and there I'd been, cutting across Regent's Park with my arms full of books as if I were the most oblivious nob in London. Damn, but I was in no mood to run. The entire month of August had been hot, and the camouflage I wore – the well-cut coat and fussy cravat of a respectable university student – was stifling. But if I didn't tuck the books away somewhere and sprint after it, I'd lose Charlie's money, and I certainly did not want to tell my wife the advance for her illustrations had been lifted from my pocket by a street rat.

The thief clearly hadn't expected me to give chase. It was of indeterminate gender, small, slender, barefoot, and wearing its own camouflage of street grime. Grime was different than filth – grime coated the skin and clothes with good, clean dirt but didn't smell of sewers or sweat. Filth stank and made people wary, therefore proper pickpockets tended to be fairly fastidious in their grooming habits under the dirt.

My annoyance grew in direct proportion to the distance we covered, and despite my longer legs, this rat had remarkable stamina. It took a turn out of the land of the quite-well-off, and darted into the dangerous territory of the very well-to-do, where the degrees of wealth ran from having one country manor to having ten. I hadn't called out for help yet – my own habit toward invisibility being too ingrained – but when the street rat sprinted toward the Langham Hotel, I finally knew how to trap it.

"Stop! Thief!"

My voice had a pleasing boom and caused people to look around for the big man they assumed must go with it. I was not overly tall – early years of hunger had likely stunted what may have been a large frame if I'd had proper feeding – but my voice had become surprisingly deep. It was menacing when I needed it to be, and authoritative enough to let me blend into the wealthy clientele of the Langham.

A slightly startled doorman, sporting the name John Hartwell on his uniform, acted without thought and grabbed my thief as she – yes, upon closer examination of delicate collar bones and elfin features, the street rat appeared to be female – attempted to slip into the hotel. I had perhaps ten seconds before Hartwell thought better of holding such a wriggly little thing and let her go; ten seconds in which to proclaim my authority over the glaring creature and retrieve Charlie's money. The shreds of my own dignity, as a pickpocket's victim, would be less simple to recover.

"Right. I'll just have my wallet back then," I said to the creature as I approached.

"I ain't got nothin' of yers," she snarled back, squirming violently in the doorman's hands.

I ignored her and met Hartwell's startled eyes. He was surprised, perhaps, that I was young and lean and didn't fit the voice I'd used to command the rat's capture. "I'll take this little vermin off your hands and remove it from your very fine establishment, if you please?" I slid into a posh, upper-crust accent – I'd been practicing such mimicry for months, and it had become frighteningly second-nature. As such things still did in the English class system, the cadence of expensive English boarding school had the desired effect. It baffled me that such a simple thing as an accent could induce a person to compliance, and yet the evidence was right in front of me.

"Right-o, Guv." Hartwell shoved the pickpocket forward, and she stumbled into my hands. She tried to wrench herself away before I could get a solid grip on her bony shoulders, but I had her spun around, one arm twisted up behind her back, before she could so much as spit, which I expected would have come next if I had been so foolish as to face her.

"All right, Rat. Out you go," I murmured into her ear as I marched her through the door and back out to the street.

"I'm no rat," she protested sharply as she attempted to bite the arm I'd wrapped across her shoulders.

"If it scurries like a rat, and squeaks like a rat, it must be a rat. The question is whether you'll escape this particular trap intact. That was my wife's money you stole, and I'll have it back now."

The girl scoffed. "'Whoever 'eard of a wife with 'er own bob? It all belongs to ye, don't it?"

"It is money she *earned*. Perhaps even you can appreciate the significance of that." I had my coin purse from the band at her waist and tucked into my trouser pocket before she felt the slightest motion. Despite having been ridiculously careless enough to get pickpocketed in the first place, my own dexterity, which had fed me for much of my early life, remained firmly habitual.

"'Ere now! That's mine ye be takin'!" Her voice screeched alarmingly, and for one quick moment I feared she would draw heroic eyes to her plight. Doormen I could reason with, but men or women of the social justice warrior class were more than I had patience for in the London heat with a wriggling pickpocket in my hands.

I leaned close to her ear and dropped my voice to a menacing snarl, adopting the most effective accent for the job. "Ye'll 'ear this once, and only once. Marylebone is mine. From Regent's Park to Mayfair and Fitzrovia, the only nimble-fingered guttersnipes that work 'ere work fer me. And since ye don't work fer me, *ye don't work 'ere.*"

The girl had frozen for exactly one second at the knife's edge in my voice, then gave up her struggle as a bad job. She wasn't afraid of me, but perhaps my accent had convinced her I wasn't quite the nob she'd first believed. My awareness of the street around us had grown more pronounced as I spoke – the sounds of horses' hooves told me the carriage that had pulled up behind me was driven by four spry Morgans, one of which was going lame. Conversations around us quickly catalogued themselves in my brain as important, like the young man gossiping with another about a scandalous baccarat game attended by the prince, or trivial, like the wife accusing her husband of appreciating another woman. And ringing above it all was the jangle of coins in a man's pocket that included the dull ring of a solid gold sovereign. I knew the rat had heard all these things as well, and I wondered if perhaps I should make a point of behaving like a tough for a few minutes each day to stay sharp.

The lunch crowd was beginning to thicken the street with the posh and powerful who regularly dined at places such as the Langham. I pulled the girl away from the hotel entrance toward Portland Place. We turned the corner to avoid a couple approaching the steps and nearly collided with a tall man in a frock coat who walked with the long stride of the very confident.

"Ringo, my dear young man! How lovely to see you!" The man's deep, cultured voice was instantly recognizable, though it had the unfortunate effect of jolting my concentration. The rat jerked her arm free, and I succeeded in catching only a bit of the collar of her shirt, which neatly disintegrated with age.

I looked up to find the enormously amused Oscar Wilde smiling down at me. "Oh dear, I do hope I didn't frighten that poor child away from whatever nefarious task you had planned for the creature," he said cheerfully.

"*She* had just successfully picked my pocket. I was merely attempting to restore a shred of my professional dignity while relieving her of the ill-gotten gain," I said as I straightened the infernal cravat.

"Your professional dignity?" Wilde ventured.

I spoke the truth with just enough humor in my tone as to render it unbelievable. "Evidently, my previous life as a thief and pickpocket didn't leave identifying marks."

Wilde's booming laughter at my apparent joke carried to the front doors of the Langham, in the direction of which he was suddenly propelling me. "Come to lunch with me. I'm meeting two other gentlemen of the storytelling persuasion, and they will wish to hear the tale of your adventure as much as I."

I thought of my books, hidden behind a bench in Regent's Park, and I thought of the long walk in the blazing midday sun to retrieve them before my planned expedition to study at the University College library, where I'd spent the past year being a respectable student of philosophy and physics, with enough history, science, and letters to keep things entertaining.

I held my hand out to shake, and it was instantly enveloped in his ridiculously large, yet remarkably gentle grip. "I'm delighted to see you again, Mr. Wilde. I was on my way to study physics, but I believe the restoration of my dignity might require a thoroughly self-effacing recounting of the day's events. Thank you for the invitation."

He clapped me on the shoulder. "Good man! Education is an admirable thing, but it is well to remember from time to time that nothing that is worth knowing can be taught. And if it assuages your conscience, I am certain there was an element of physics at play in the encounter with your thief."

I chuckled as I recalled an image of the street rat dropping off a wall, tumbling down an embankment, and leaping a leashed bulldog that turned and snapped at her heels. She was resourceful and intrepid – qualities I rarely had the occasion to admire among my recent acquaintances.

"Indeed, there was." I looked back over my shoulder for the young thief I knew was long gone, and then allowed myself to be directed back into the elegant foyer of the Langham Hotel.

An Urchin of Means is available on all platforms.